*Tomcat Darius the Wizard*

**20 Kurzgeschichten**
*(Englisch / Deutsch) in Dialogform mit Übungen*

**von**

**Bernhard Ludwig©**

Bibliografische Information der Deutschen Nationalbibliothek: Die Deutsche Nationalbibliothek verzeichnet diese Publikation in der Deutschen Nationalbibliografie; detaillierte bibliografische Daten sind im Internet über dnb.dnb.de abrufbar.

Verlag: BoD · Books on Demand GmbH, In de Tarpen 42, 22848 Norderstedt

Druck: Libri Plureos GmbH, Friedensallee 273, 22763 Hamburg

ISBN: 978-3-7597-2417-5

# Inhaltsverzeichnis

# 1 Darius and the Magic Potion

&lt;Derek, a considerate husband, has come to Darius to ask him to make a magic potion for his ill wife&gt;

**Derek:** Darius! I need your help!

&lt;Darius is smiling&gt;

**Darius:** Derek, you again! You surely need another fertilizer for your flowers, right? But as I told you some days ago, I'm so busy these days that I'm not able to make you any.

**Derek:** No! I don't need anything like that! My wife is ill! She's got a temperature and coughs very often. I beg you to make me a magic potion to heal her disease as soon as possible!

**Darius:** Oh dear, this is bad news! Of course, I'll help you the best I can! I'll make one for you right now!

# 1 Darius und der Zaubertrank

&lt;Derek, ein fürsorglicher Ehemann, ist zu Darius gekommen, um ihn darum zu bitten, einen magischen Trank für seine kranke Frau zuzubereiten&gt;

**Derek:** Darius! Ich brauche deine Hilfe!

&lt;Darius lächelt&gt;

**Darius:** Derek, du schon wieder! Du brauchst sicherlich wieder einen Dünger für deine Blumen, richtig? Aber wie ich dir bereits vor ein paar Tagen sagte, bin ich dieser Tage sehr beschäftigt, sodass es mir nicht möglich ist, dir welche zu machen.

**Derek:** Nein! Ich brauche nichts dergleichen! Meine Frau ist krank! Sie hat Fieber und hustet sehr oft. Ich flehe dich an, mir einen magischen Trank zuzubereiten, um ihre Krankheit so schnell wie möglich zu heilen!

**Darius:** Oje, das sind schlechte Neuigkeiten! Selbstverständlich, ich werde dir so gut ich kann helfen! Ich werde dir umgehend einen zubereiten!

<Darius is mixing different plants with colourful fluids now. A few minutes have passed. Now he's filling a red fluid into a little bottle>

**Darius:** Done! Here's the magic potion for your suffering wife! Please make her drink the whole bottle. After that, she should get better soon.

<Derek is going down on his knees ...>

**Derek:** Thank you so much, Darius! Without your help, my wife could have died ...

<Darius is touching Derek's shoulders>

**Darius:** There's no need to say thank you.

<Derek is smiling>

**Derek:** I should leave now … Thank you, Darius ...

<Derek is running to his house to give his wife the potion>

**Derek:** Darling! Darius has made a potion which will surely help you!

<Darius mischt nun verschiedene Pflanzen mit bunten Flüssigkeiten. Ein paar Minuten sind vergangen. Nun füllt er eine rote Flüssigkeit in eine kleine Flasche>

**Darius:** Fertig! Hier ist der magische Trank für deine leidende Frau! Bitte bringe sie dazu, die gesamte Flasche zu trinken. Danach sollte sie sich bald wieder erholen.

<Derek kniet nieder ...>

**Derek:** Ich danke dir so sehr, Darius! Ohne deine Hilfe hätte meine Frau sterben können ...

<Darius berührt Dereks Schulter>

**Darius:** Es gibt keinen Grund, sich zu bedanken.

<Derek lächelt>

**Derek:** Ich sollte nun gehen … Danke, Darius ...

<Derek rennt zu seinem Haus, um seiner Frau den Trank zu geben>

**Derek:** Liebling! Darius hat einen Trank zubereitet, der dir sicherlich helfen wird!

**Erica:** T-thank you ...

**Derek:** Here you are.

<Erica is drinking the potion now. A few minutes have passed. Derek is waiting for his wife to tell him if the potion is helpful>

**Erica:** I'm feeling much better now ...

<Derek is jumping up and down while laughing>

**Derek:** I'm so happy to hear this, love! Darius is the best wizard of all wizards!

**Erica:** I'm so glad that the pain is getting weaker ... It has been horrible! I'd like to do something to express my gratitude to him.

**Derek:** Yes, let's think up something special!

**Erica:** D-danke ...

**Derek:** Hier, bitte.

<Erica trinkt nun den Trank. Ein paar Minuten sind vergangen. Derek wartet darauf, dass seine Frau ihm sagt, ob der Trank hilfreich ist>

**Erica:** Ich fühle mich nun viel besser ...

<Derek springt auf und ab, während er lacht>

**Derek:** Ich bin so glücklich, das zu hören, mein Liebes! Darius ist der beste Zauberer von allen Zauberern!

**Erica:** Ich bin so froh, dass der Schmerz nachlässt ... Es ist fürchterlich gewesen! Ich möchte etwas tun, um ihm meine Dankbarkeit auszudrücken.

**Derek:** Ja, lass uns etwas Besonderes einfallen!

## 2 The Love Spell

&lt;Darius is sitting on a tree stump, which stands in a meadow with a lot of beautiful, colourful flowers. It's spring, and he's in a very good mood. He's reading an old book, which contains a lot of different spells&gt;

**Darius:** I love to read this good old book. My master gave it to me after I had finished my studies ...

&lt;Darius notices that he's being observed by somebody. Darius to himself ...&gt;

**Darius:** I can feel that somebody is watching me right now. Who could it be? Derek? No, I think he's working in the garden at this time. A creature from the nearby forest? Perhaps, but this would make no sense at all. Why would it be interested in an old wizard who's reading a book?
A book … Ah, that could be the reason. Maybe somebody wants to learn some spells ...  I'd better be very careful now.

&lt;Behold, a young man is jumping out of a bush!&gt;

# 2 Der Liebeszauber

&lt;Darius sitzt gerade auf einem Baumstumpf, der auf einer Wiese mit vielen schönen, bunten Blumen steht. Es ist Frühling und er ist in sehr guter Stimmung. Er liest ein altes Buch, das viele verschiedene Zauber enthält&gt;

**Darius:** Ich liebe es, dieses gute alte Buch zu lesen. Mein Meister gab es mir, nachdem ich mein Studium beendet hatte …

&lt;Darius bemerkt, dass er von jemandem beobachtet wird. Darius zu sich selbst …&gt;

**Darius:** Ich kann fühlen, dass mich jemand gerade beobachtet. Wer könnte es sein? Derek? Nein, ich denke, er arbeitet um diese Zeit im Garten. Eine Kreatur aus dem nahegelegenen Wald? Vielleicht, aber das würde überhaupt keinen Sinn ergeben. Warum sollte sie sich für einen alten Zauberer interessieren, der ein Buch liest?
Ein Buch … Ah, das könnte der Grund sein. Vielleicht will jemand ein paar Zauber lernen ... Ich sollte nun besser sehr vorsichtig sein.

&lt;Siehe, ein junger Mann springt aus einem Busch hervor!&gt;

**Young Man:** Hey, tiny wizard! What's that book? May I have a look at it?

**Darius:** Who are you? I've never seen you before ...

<The young man is smiling while remaining silent>

**Darius:** Please leave me alone.

<Behold, the young man is turning into a stinky, big troll! Darius is starting to cast a spell, but the big troll knocks Darius out, takes the book, and disappears in the forest>

**Big Troll:** Now that I've got the book full of spells, I can make that beautiful troll girl love me!

<The big troll is smiling>

**Big Troll:** Rachel! Rachel! Where are you, my dear Rachel? Ah, over there she is!

<Now the big troll is starting to cast a love spell>

**Junger Mann:** Hey, winziger Zauberer! Was ist das für ein Buch? Darf ich es mir mal ansehen?

**Darius:** Wer bist du? Ich habe dich noch nie zuvor gesehen ...

<Der junge Mann lächelt, während er schweigt>

**Darius:** Bitte lass mich alleine.

<Siehe, der junge Mann verwandelt sich in einen stinkenden, großen Troll! Darius beginnt einen Zauber zu sprechen, aber der große Troll schlägt Darius k.o., nimmt das Buch und verschwindet im Wald>

**Großer Troll:** Nun, da ich das Buch voller Zauber habe, kann ich das schöne Trollmädchen dazu bringen, mich zu lieben!

<Der große Troll lächelt>

**Großer Troll:** Rachel! Rachel! Wo bist du, meine liebe Rachel? Ah, dort drüben ist sie!

<Nun beginnt der große Troll einen Liebeszauber zu sprechen>

**Darius:** Stop that at once!

\<The big troll is ignoring Darius\>

**Darius:** I'll burn your butt with a nice fireball!

\<After Darius had cast a spell, a mighty fireball hit the buttocks of the big troll. Now Darius is laughing while the big troll is running away, holding his buttocks\>

**Trollgirl:** Thank you so much, Darius, for stopping that mad guy!

\<Darius is laughing\>

**Darius:** No problem! But something is strange about him … The first time I saw him, he had the same appearance as a young man … You know that trolls aren't able to change their appearance.

**Trollgirl:** Of course. Some days ago, when I saw him, he babbled that an old man called Unandex had made a potion for him.

\<Darius is shocked\>

**Darius:** Hör sofort auf damit!

<Der große Troll ignoriert Darius>

**Darius:** Ich werde deinen Hintern mit einem schönen Feuerball verbrennen!

<Nachdem Darius einen Zauber gesprochen hatte, traf ein mächtiger Feuerball das Gesäß des großen Trolls. Jetzt, lacht Darius, während der große Troll davon rennt und sich an das Gesäß greift>

**Trollmädchen:** Ich danke dir so sehr, Darius, dass du diesen Verrückten gestoppt hast!

<Darius lacht>

**Darius:** Kein Problem! Aber etwas an ihm ist seltsam … Das erste Mal, als ich ihn sah, hatte er das gleiche Aussehen wie ein junger Mann … Du weißt ja, dass Trolle ihr Aussehen nicht verändern können.

**Trollmädchen:** Natürlich. Als ich ihn vor ein paar Tagen sah, faselte er, dass ein alter Mann namens Unandex einen Trank für ihn hergestellt habe.

<Darius ist geschockt>

**Darius:** Unandex?!

**Trollgirl:** You know him?

**Darius:** Indeed, I do … Unandex is a very evil man who tries to collect as many souls as he can to use them for his black magic … I thought that he died fifty years ago …When you see the big troll again, please tell him who Unandex is and that he must be careful!

**Trollgirl:** Oh dear … Yes, I'll tell him as soon as possible.

**Darius:** Thank you! It's my duty to inform the Queen about Unandex. Goodbye!

**Trollgril:** Goodbye!

**Darius:** Unandex?!

**Trollmädchen:** Du kennst ihn?

**Darius:** In der Tat, das tue ich … Unandex ist ein sehr böser Mann, der versucht, so viele Seelen wie möglich zu sammeln, um sie für seine schwarze Magie zu verwenden … Ich dachte, er wäre vor fünfzig Jahren gestorben …Wenn du den großen Troll wiedersiehst, sage ihm bitte, wer Unandex ist, und dass er sehr vorsichtig sein soll!

**Trollmädchen:** Oje … Ja, ich werde es ihm schnellstmöglich sagen.

**Darius:** Ich danke dir! Es ist meine Pflicht, der Königin von Unandex zu berichten. Tschüss!

**Trollmädchen:** Tschüss!

# 3 Lord of Irnovoire

<The townspeople are shouting and crying loudly because they're being attacked. Darius is going for a walk in the forest and can't hear it. Derek is looking for him despairingly at the moment>

**Derek:** Where are you, Darius? Something horrible is happening in town! Darius!!! He's not at home at the moment … Where could he have gone?

<Suddenly, a little bird has appeared. Derek is astonished>

**Derek:** Where have you come from?

**Little Bird:** Forest! Go to the forest!

**Derek:** To the forest? Why should I go to the forest?

**Little Bird:** Forest! Go to the forest!

**Derek:** Is Darius in the forest? Do you mean that?

**Little Bird:** Darius, in the forest!

**Derek:** Thank you so much, my little friend!

# 3 Fürst von Irnovoire

&lt;Die Stadtbewohner schreien und weinen laut, weil sie gerade angegriffen werden. Darius spaziert im Wald und kann es nicht hören. Derek sucht im Moment verzweifelt nach ihm&gt;

**Derek:** Wo bist du, Darius? Etwas Schreckliches passiert in der Stadt! Darius!!! Er ist momentan nicht zu Hause … Wo könnte er hingegangen sein?

&lt;Plötzlich ist ein kleiner Vogel erschienen. Derek ist verwundert&gt;

**Derek:** Von wo bist du hergekommen?

**Kleiner Vogel:** Wald! Geh zum Wald!

**Derek:** Zum Wald? Warum sollte ich zum Wald gehen?

**Kleiner Vogel:** Wald! Geh zum Wald!

**Derek:** Ist Darius im Wald? Meinst du das?

**Kleiner Vogel:** Darius, im Wald!

**Derek:** Ich danke dir so sehr, mein kleiner Freund!

&lt;Behold, the little bird has disappeared. Derek is running into the forest now&gt;

**Derek:** There you are! Darius!

**Darius:** What's the matter, Derek?

**Derek:** The town is being attacked by terrifying creatures! Skeletons, black shadows, necromancers ...

**Darius:** I'll go to the town immediately and try to support the town guard!

**Derek:** Perfect! I must go and get my axe, and then it's time to kill some of the monsters!

**Darius:** Alright, but be careful, please!

**Derek:** Sure!

&lt;Darius has just arrived in town&gt;

**Darius:** Ah, it's you, Lord of Irnovoire!

**Lord of Irnovoire:** My dear Darius! It's been a while ... You won't defeat me again ...

<Siehe, der kleine Vogel ist verschwunden. Derek rennt nun in den Wald>

**Derek:** Da bist du! Darius!

**Darius:** Was ist los, Derek?

**Derek:** Die Stadt wird von entsetzlichen Monstern angegriffen! Skelette, schwarze Schatten, Nekromanten ...

**Darius:** Ich werde sofort zur Stadt gehen und versuchen, die Stadtwache zu unterstützen!

**Derek:** Perfekt! Ich muss meine Axt holen gehen und dann ist es an der Zeit, ein paar der Monster zu töten!

**Darius:** Alles klar, aber sei bitte vorsichtig!

**Derek:** Sicher!

<Darius ist soeben in der Stadt angekommen>

**Darius:** Ah, du bist es, Fürst von Irnovoire!

**Fürst von Irnovoire:** Mein lieber Darius! Es ist eine Weile her ... Du wirst mich nicht noch einmal besiegen ...

&lt;The Lord of Irnovoire is swinging his long, black sword now&gt;

**Darius:** Everybody, sing our glorious hymn!

&lt;Everybody is confused and staring at Darius&gt;

**Darius:** Just do it!

&lt;The Lord of Irnovoire is laughing loudly&gt;

**Lord of Irnovoire:** What are you trying to do, Darius? Kill them!

&lt;While the townspeople are singing, Darius is holding his magic wand towards the sky and casting a spell. Behold, purple lightnings are appearing and striking the townspeople&gt;

**Lord of Irnovoire:** You're killing your friends? That's OUR job!

&lt;Darius is smiling. Now a loud thunder can be heard, and thousands of lightnings are coming out of the townspeople and striking all monsters&gt;

**Lord of Irnovoire:** No! My lovely monsters!

<Der Fürst von Irnovoire schwingt nun sein langes, schwarzes Schwert>

**Darius:** Ihr alle, singt unsere glorreiche Hymne!

<Alle sind verdutzt und starren Darius an>

**Darius:** Tut es einfach!

<Der Fürst von Irnovoire lacht laut>

**Fürst von Irnovoire:** Was versuchst du zu tun, Darius? Tötet sie!

<Während die Stadtbewohner singen, hält Darius seinen Zauberstab gen Himmel und spricht einen Zauber. Siehe, lila Blitze erscheinen und schlagen in die Stadtbewohner ein>

**Fürst von Irnovoire:** Du tötest deine Freunde? Das ist UNSERE Aufgabe!

<Darius lächelt. Nun kann man einen lauten Donner hören und Tausende von Blitzen kommen aus den Stadtbewohnern heraus und schlagen in alle Monster ein>

**Fürst von Irnovoire:** Nein! Meine lieben Monster!

<Now Darius is holding his magic wand towards the Lord of Irnovoire, and with a loud thunder, a dazzling white lightning is striking the Lord of Irnovoire>

**Lord of Irnovoire:** No!!!

<Behold, the Lord of Irnovoire has disappeared, and all the monsters with him. All the townspeople are laughing and praising Darius>

<Nun hält Darius seinen Zauberstab gen Fürst von Irnovoire und mit einem lauten Donner schlägt ein blendend weißer Blitz in den Fürst von Irnovoire ein>

**Fürst von Irnovoire:** Nein!!!

<Siehe, der Fürst von Irnovoire ist verschwunden und alle Monster mit ihm. Alle Stadtbewohner lachen und loben Darius>

# 4 Darius' Double

<Darius and his cousin Lila are talking about the good old times while drinking a cup of tea in the living room. While Derek is working in his beloved garden, he notices a tomcat that looks just like Darius!>

**Derek:** Who's that? He looks like Darius, but this can't be, because his cousin has come for a visit, and as far as I know, they're at Darius' home right now.

<Now the tomcat is putting money into a chest>

**Derek:** He seems to be pretty rich ...

<Now the tomcat is burying the chest>

**Derek:** Interesting … I must tell Darius what has happened!

<It's the day after the strange happenings. Derek has just told Darius about the rich tomcat and the treasure chest>

# 4 Darius' Doppelgänger

<Darius und seine Cousine, Lila, sprechen gerade über die guten alten Zeiten, während sie eine Tasse Tee im Wohnzimmer trinken. Während Derek in seinem geliebten Garten arbeitet, bemerkt er einen Kater, der genauso aussieht wie Darius!>

**Derek:** Wer ist das? Er sieht wie Darius aus, aber das kann nicht sein, weil seine Cousine zu Besuch gekommen ist, und soviel ich weiß, sind sie jetzt bei Darius.

<Nun legt der Kater Geld in eine Truhe>

**Derek:** Er scheint ziemlich reich zu sein ...

<Nun vergräbt der Kater die Truhe>

**Derek:** Interessant … Ich muss Darius erzählen, was geschehen ist!

<Es ist der Tag nach den seltsamen Geschehnissen. Derek hat Darius soeben von dem reichen Kater und der Schatztruhe erzählt>

**Darius:** That's suspicious! Maybe somebody tries to earn money with fake potions or something like that while posing as me.

**Derek:** Yes, this could be!

**Darius:** Let's set a trap for him!

<Darius and Derek are deliberating on a good trap for the tomcat now. A few days have passed. Derek is buying some things at the market, while Darius is hiding himself>

**Derek:** Isn't there a stall where I can get some magic potions? I really need some! Isn't there a wizard or alchemist in town?

<Behold! The tomcat has just shown up, and now he is calling quietly ...>

**Tomcat:** Hey, you! I've got what you need! The best potions you can get!

**Derek:** Ah, that's great! I'd like to buy two of them! You are Darius, right?

**Darius:** Das ist verdächtig! Vielleicht versucht jemand, mit gefälschten Tränken oder so etwas in der Art Geld zu verdienen, während er sich als mich ausgibt.

**Derek:** Ja, das könnte sein!

**Darius:** Lass uns ihm eine Falle stellen!

<Darius und Derek beraten nun über eine gute Falle für den Kater. Ein paar Tage sind vergangen. Derek kauft gerade ein paar Dinge auf dem Marktplatz, während Darius sich versteckt>

**Derek:** Gibt es keinen Verkaufsstand, wo ich ein paar magische Tränke bekommen kann? Ich brauche dringend welche! Gibt es hier keinen Zauberer oder Alchemisten in der Stadt?

<Siehe da! Der Kater ist gerade aufgetaucht, und nun ruft er leise ...>

**Kater:** Hey, du! Ich habe, was du brauchst! Die besten Tränke, die du bekommen kannst!

**Derek:** Ah, das ist großartig! Ich möchte gerne zwei davon kaufen! Du bist Darius, richtig?

**Tomcat:** Sure! Yes, I am! You've already heard from me?

<Now Darius appears and grabs the tomcat by his coat>

**Darius:** I am the only wizard here! And I am the true Darius!

<The tomcat is confused>

**Tomcat:** D-Darius?!

**Darius:** Yes, stop posing as me, or I have to call the town guard!

**Tomcat:** Please, don't arrest me! I'll stop it! I promise!

**Kater:** Sicher! Ja, das bin ich! Du hast bereits von mir gehört?

<Nun erscheint Darius und greift den Kater am Mantel>

**Darius:** Ich bin der einzige Zauberer hier! Und ich bin der wahre Darius!

<Der Kater ist verdutzt>

**Kater:** D-Darius?!

**Darius:** Ja, hör auf dich als mich auszugeben, oder ich muss die Stadtwache rufen!

**Kater:** Bitte, verhafte mich nicht! Ich werde damit aufhören! Versprochen!

# 5 Solar Eclipse

<Darius is practising some new spells in his garden. Some little imps are watching him while enjoying some cool drinks>

**Darius:** So … Now let's try a mighty ice wall!

<A mighty ice wall has appeared>

**Darius:** That's nice! This can be used to protect me or others. Alright! Now I'll conjure a little thunderstorm!

<A little thunderstorm is starting>

**Darius:** Ok, stop!

<The little thunderstorm is disappearing now>

**Darius:** So ... Now I'll summon a shadow demon!

<A shadow demon has appeared. The little imps are applauding and laughing>

# 5 Sonnenfinsternis

<Darius übt gerade neue Zauber in seinem Garten. Ein paar kleine Kobolde schauen ihm zu, während sie ein paar kühle Getränke genießen>

**Darius:** So … Nun, lasst mich eine mächtige Eiswand versuchen!

<Eine mächtige Eiswand ist erschienen>

**Darius:** Das ist schön! Diese kann dazu verwendet werden, mich oder andere zu schützen. Alles klar! Nun werde ich ein kleines Gewitter herbeirufen!

<Ein kleines Gewitter beginnt>

**Darius:** Ok, stopp!

<Das kleine Gewitter verschwindet nun>

**Darius:** So ... Nun werde ich einen Schattendämon herbeirufen!

<Ein Schattendämon ist erschienen. Die kleinen Kobolde applaudieren und lachen>

**Darius:** That's impressive, isn't it?

<Behold! The shadow demon is casting a spell to eclipse the sun>

**Darius:** Stop! Disappear, shadow demon!

<The shadow demon is laughing>

**Darius:** Oh no, I forgot to bind it! I've no control over him!

<Now the little imps are screaming. Derek is sitting in his garden ...>

**Derek:** A solar eclipse! Darling, look!

**Darius:** How can I ban the demon? ... Yes! I've got an idea! You, imps! Please intensify my ban spell! Afterwards, you'll receive a big chocolate gateau, all right?

<The imps are dancing and laughing now. Darius is starting to cast the ban spell while the demon is distracted. After Darius had cast the spell, a small gate has appeared. The demon is being sucked into it. A few seconds have passed>

**Darius:** Das ist beeindruckend, nicht wahr?

<Siehe! Der Schattendämon spricht einen Zauber, um die Sonne zu verdunkeln>

**Darius:** Stopp! Verschwinde, Schattendämon!

<Der Schattendämon lacht>

**Darius:** Oh nein, ich vergaß, ihn zu binden! Ich habe keine Macht über ihn!

<Nun schreien die kleinen Kobolde. Derek sitzt gerade im Garten ...>

**Derek:** Eine Sonnenfinsternis! Liebling, schau!

**Darius:** Wie kann ich den Dämon verbannen? ... Ja! Ich habe eine Idee! Ihr, Kobolde! Bitte verstärkt meinen Bannzauber! Nach dem hier, werdet ihr eine Schokoladentorte bekommen, alles klar?

<Die Kobolde tanzen und lachen nun. Darius beginnt den Bannzauber zu sprechen, während der Dämon abgelenkt ist. Nachdem Darius den Zauber gesprochen hatte, ist ein kleines Tor erschienen. Der Dämon wird in es hineingezogen. Wenige Sekunden sind vergangen>

\<The demon has disappeared>

**Darius:** We did it!

\<The imps are cheering>

<Der Dämon ist verschwunden>

**Darius:** Wir haben es geschafft!

<Die Kobolde jubeln>

# 6 The Possessed Girl

&lt;It's a cold evening in winter. Darius is sitting in front of his fireplace while reading a letter from his old friend. Now Darius is hearing a girl's voice&gt;

**Girl:** Your time has come … You will be sacrificed for my lord …

**Darius:** Who are you? Where are you? I can't see you anywhere …

**Girl:** I'm nowhere … I'm in the darkness … I devote myself to my lord …

**Darius:** Who's your lord? Do I know him? Why do you want to sacrifice me?

&lt;The girl is laughing&gt;

**Darius:** Answer me! I want you to answer me!

&lt;The girl's voice is disappearing. Darius can't understand what the girl is saying&gt;

# 6 Das besessene Mädchen

<Es ist ein kalter Abend im Winter. Darius sitzt gerade vor seinem Kamin, während er einen Brief seines alten Freundes liest. Nun hört Darius die Stimme eines Mädchens>

**Mädchen:** Deine Zeit ist gekommen … Du wirst meinem Herrn geopfert werden ...

**Darius:** Wer bist du? Wo bist du? Ich kann dich nirgendwo sehen ...

**Mädchen:** Ich bin nirgendwo … Ich bin in der Dunkelheit … Ich widme mein Leben meinem Herrn ...

**Darius:** Wer ist dein Herr? Kenne ich ihn? Warum willst du mich opfern?

<Das Mädchen lacht>

**Darius:** Antworte mir! Ich will, dass du mir antwortest!

<Die Stimme des Mädchens verschwindet. Darius kann nicht verstehen, was das Mädchen sagt>

**Darius:** What was that? I must find out who this girl is! I should try to use a special spell that my master once taught me.

<Darius is casting the spell>

**Darius:** It works! I can see her ... That is ... I can't believe it! That is farmer Arius' daughter! I'd better go to his farm immediately!

<Darius is running as fast as he can now. A few minutes have passed. He's arrived at farmer Arius' farm>

**Darius:** Arius! I need to talk to you! It's urgent!

<Arius has just opened the door>

**Arius:** Ah, my friend Darius! Can I help you?

<Now Darius is telling him what happened>

**Arius:** Oh dear! I don't know anything ... What's wrong with my dear daughter?

**Darius:** Is she at home?

**Darius:** Was war das? Ich muss herausfinden, wer dieses Mädchen ist! Ich sollte versuchen, einen speziellen Zauber zu benutzen, den mich mein Meister einst lehrte.

<Darius spricht den Zauber>

**Darius:** Es funktioniert! Ich kann sie sehen … Das ist … Ich kann es nicht glauben! Das ist Bauer Arius' Tochter! Ich sollte besser sofort zu seinem Bauernhof gehen!

<Darius rennt nun so schnell er kann. Wenige Minuten sind vergangen. Er hat den Bauernhof von Bauer Arius erreicht>

**Darius:** Arius! Ich muss mit dir sprechen! Es ist dringend!

<Arius hat gerade die Tür geöffnet>

**Arius:** Ah, mein Freund, Darius! Kann ich dir helfen?

<Jetzt erzählt Darius ihm, was geschehen ist>

**Arius:** Oje! Ich weiß überhaupt nichts … Was stimmt mit meiner lieben Tochter nicht?

**Darius:** Ist sie zu Hause?

**Arius:** No, she said that she would visit her best friend Lina.

**Darius:** So, please lead me to Lina's home.

**Arius:** Sure, follow me!

<Arius and Darius have just reached Lina's home>

**Arius:** Over there's Evelyn, my daughter!

<Evelyn is watching them with a frightening facial expression>

**Arius:** Evelyn, what are you doing there?

<Evelyn is smiling>

**Darius:** She's possessed! I can feel it! Arius, stay here, please!

**Arius:** Alright!

**Darius:** I'm here to set you free, Evelyn!

<Evelyn is laughing while taking a knife>

**Arius:** Nein, sie sagte, sie würde ihre beste Freundin Lina besuchen.

**Darius:** So, führe mich bitte zu Linas Zuhause.

**Arius:** Sicher, folge mir!

\<Arius und Darius haben soeben Linas Zuhause erreicht>

**Arius:** Dort drüben ist Evelyn, meine Tochter!

\<Evelyn sieht sie mit einem furchterregenden Gesichtsausdruck an>

**Arius:** Evelyn, was machst du dort?

\<Evelyn lächelt>

**Darius:** Sie ist besessen! Ich kann es fühlen! Arius, bleib bitte hier!

**Arius:** Alles klar!

**Darius:** Ich bin hier, um dich zu befreien, Evelyn!

\<Evelyn lacht, während sie ein Messer zückt>

**Arius:** Darius, be careful!

<Darius has casted a spell, and behold, colourful rays of light have hit Evelyn>

**Evelyn:** No!! Aaah ...

**Arius:** Evelyn!

<Arius is running to Evelyn now, and Darius is hearing a voice saying ...>

**Voice:** Darius, sooner or later, I'll get you!

**Darius:** Lord of Irnovoire?!

<The voice is gone>

**Evelyn:** I'm fine ... What happened? I can't remember anything ... Why am I lying here on the ground?

**Arius:** Don't worry, everything is fine ...

<Now Darius is telling Evelyn everything that's just happened>

**Arius:** Darius, sei vorsichtig!

<Darius hat einen Zauber gesprochen und siehe, Evelyn haben bunte Lichtstrahlen getroffen>

**Evelyn:** Nein!! Aaah ...

**Arius:** Evelyn!

<Arius rennt nun zu Evelyn und Darius hört eine Stimme sagen ...>

**Stimme:** Darius, früher oder später werde ich dich kriegen!

**Darius:** Fürst von Irnovoire?!

<Die Stimme ist fort>

**Evelyn:** Mir geht es gut … Was ist geschehen? Ich kann mich an nichts erinnern ... Warum liege ich hier auf dem Boden?

**Arius:** Mach dir keine Sorgen, alles ist gut ...

<Nun erzählt Darius Evelyn alles, was gerade geschehen ist>

# 7 The Swindler

**Darius:** Ah, it's so nice … lying in the sun with a cool drink and cooling my legs in the lake ...

<Darius has come to a marvellous, little lake in the forest>

**Darius:** Good morning, Mister Gnome! How are you today?

**Mister Gnome:** Everything's fine, thanks! I see that you're enjoying the beautiful day!

**Darius:** Of course, it's been raining a lot lately. I don't want to miss such a good opportunity to spend a day at the lake!

<Mister Gnome is laughing>

**Mister Gnome:** Sure! Unfortunately, I can't do the same because I need to buy a new magic robe for my son. As you know, he's going to study magic at the academy.

**Darius:** Why don't you buy one of my robes?

# 7 Der Betrüger

**Darius:** Ah, es ist so schön … in der Sonne mit einem kühlen Trunk zu liegen und meine Beine im See zu kühlen …

<Darius ist zu einem wundervollen, kleinen See im Wald gekommen>

**Darius:** Guten Morgen, Herr Gnom! Wie geht es Ihnen heute?

**Herr Gnom:** Alles gut, danke! Ich sehe, dass Sie den schönen Tag genießen!

**Darius:** Natürlich, es hat in letzter Zeit viel geregnet. Ich will mir solch eine gute Gelegenheit, einen Tag am See zu verbringen, nicht entgehen lassen!

<Herr Gnom lacht>

**Herr Gnom:** Sicher! Unglücklicherweise kann ich nicht dasselbe tun, weil ich eine neue magische Robe für meinen Sohn kaufen muss. Wie Sie wissen, wird er bald an der Akademie Magie studieren.

**Darius:** Warum kaufen Sie nicht eine meiner Roben?

**Mister Gnome:** Well, it's just that your robes are more expensive than the ones from that merchant.

**Darius:** Who's that merchant?

**Mister Gnome:** I don't know his name, but he sells his goods on the hill over there.

**Darius:** Would you mind if I came with you?

**Mister Gnome:** Of course not!

<Darius and Mister Gnome are walking to the merchant now>

**Darius:** I can't believe it! He again!

<The merchant is the tomcat that sold magic goods while posing as Darius some time ago>

**Tomcat:** Oh no! Please forgive me! I won't do it again, I promise!

**Darius:** Of course, you said the same thing last time. I don't trust you anymore! I'll take you to the town guard!

**Herr Gnom:** Nun, es ist ganz einfach so, dass ihre Roben teurer sind als die jenes Händlers.

**Darius:** Wer ist jener Händler?

**Herr Gnom:** Ich kenne seinen Namen nicht, aber er verkauft seine Güter auf dem Hügel dort.

**Darius:** Würde es Ihnen etwas ausmachen, wenn ich mitkomme?

**Herr Gnom:** Natürlich nicht!

<Darius und Herr Gnom gehen nun zum Händler>

**Darius:** Ich kann es nicht glauben! Er wieder!

<Der Händler ist der Kater, der vor einiger Zeit magische Güter verkaufte, während er sich als Darius ausgab>

**Kater:** Oh nein! Bitte vergib mir! Ich werde es nicht wieder machen, ich verspreche es!

**Darius:** Natürlich, das Gleiche hast du letztes Mal gesagt. Ich vertraue dir nicht mehr! Ich werde dich zur Stadtwache bringen!

**Tomcat:** No, please, not to the town guard! I'll become a better tomcat! I'll do everything you ask me to do!

**Darius:** Hm, an assistant for my current alchemy project would really help me …

**Tomcat:** Alchemy? Sure, I'm your tomcat! I always take my little alchemy kit with me. Have a look!

<Now the tomcat is showing Darius his little alchemy kit>

**Darius:** Wow! I'm pretty impressed!

<The tomcat is smiling>

**Tomcat:** Ok, then lead me to your laboratory, and I'll help you as well as I can!

**Darius:** Great! Follow me!

<Now Darius and the tomcat are working pretty hard in Darius' laboratory>

**Kater:** Nein, bitte nicht zur Stadtwache! Ich werde ein besserer Kater werden! Ich werde alles tun, um was du mich bittest!

**Darius:** Hm, ein Assistent für mein momentanes Alchemie-Projekt würde mir sehr helfen …

**Kater:** Alchemie? Sicher, ich bin dein Kater! Ich habe immer meinen kleinen Alchemiekasten bei mir. Hier, schau!

<Jetzt zeigt der Kater Darius seinen kleinen Alchemiekasten>

**Darius:** Wow! Ich bin recht beeindruckt!

<Der Kater lächelt>

**Kater:** Ok, dann führe mich zu deinem Laboratorium und ich werde dir, so gut ich kann, helfen!

**Darius:** Großartig! Folge mir!

<Nun arbeiten Darius und der Kater ziemlich hart in Darius' Laboratorium>

## 8 The Family Heirloom

<It's a warm night in summer. The stars are twinkling. While Darius is sleeping in his bedroom, somebody is knocking on his door>

**Darius:** Hm … I'm so tired … Who could this be? Maybe it's Derek who wants to show me a new flower or something like that ... Derek?

**Voice:** Please, help me! There's a ghost!

**Darius:** Well, that's not Derek … A ghost? I think I should put on my clothes and open the door.

<Now Darius is opening the door. A big elephant lady from another country is standing in front of Darius' house>

**Darius:** Ah, you are from the country 'Terra Elephantorum Magicorum'! I haven't been there for a while ... It's a pleasure to meet you!

**The Elephant Lady:** Oh, you really know a lot! It's a pleasure for me, as well! Well, my name's Babette.

# 8 Das Familienerbstück

&lt;Es ist eine warme Nacht im Sommer. Die Sterne funkeln. Während Darius in seinem Schlafzimmer schläft, klopft jemand an der Tür&gt;

**Darius:** Hm … Ich bin so müde … Wer könnte das sein? Vielleicht ist es Derek, der mir eine neue Blume oder so etwas zeigen will … Derek?

**Stimme:** Bitte helft mir! Da ist ein Geist!

**Darius:** Nun, das ist nicht Derek … Ein Geist? Ich denke, ich sollte mich anziehen und die Tür öffnen.

&lt;Nun öffnet Darius die Tür. Eine große Elefantendame aus einem anderen Land steht vor Darius' Tür&gt;

**Darius:** Ah, Ihr kommt aus dem Land „Terra Elephantorum Magicorum"! Ich bin schon eine Weile nicht mehr dort gewesen ... Ich bin sehr erfreut, Euch kennenzulernen!

**Die Elefantendame:** Oh, Ihr wisst wirklich viel! Ich bin auch sehr erfreut, Euch kennenzulernen! Also, mein Name ist Babette.

**Darius:** My name's Darius. Well, how can I help you?

**Babette:** Well, I inherited a house in this town. After I had stayed there for a few hours, suddenly, a ghost that looked like my dead grandpa appeared and said, 'Where's my tea service?', over and over again.

<Darius is confused>

**Darius:** Well … I see ... Please lead me to your house. It's important that I see the ghost myself.

**Babette:** Thank you! Sure, let's go!

<Babette has just grabbed Darius' paw. Now she's running with him to her house>

**Babette:** Here we are!

**Darius:** I'm a bit dizzy … Where's the door?

<Babette is laughing while she's opening the door. Darius has entered the house. A few minutes have passed. Behold! The ghost is appearing>

**Darius:** There, I can see the ghost!

**Darius:** Mein Name ist Darius. Nun, wie kann ich dir helfen?

**Babette:** Also, ich habe ein Haus in der Stadt geerbt. Nachdem ich mich ein paar Stunden dort aufgehalten hatte, erschien plötzlich ein Geist, der wie mein Opa aussah, und sagte: „Wo ist mein Teeservice?", immer und immer wieder.

<Darius ist verdutzt>

**Darius:** Nun … ich verstehe ... Bitte führe mich zu deinem Haus. Es ist wichtig, dass ich den Geist selbst sehe.

**Babette:** Danke! Sicher, lass uns gehen!

<Babette hat gerade Darius' Pfote ergriffen. Nun rennt sie mit ihm zu ihrem Haus>

**Babette:** Hier sind wir!

**Darius:** Mir ist etwas schwindelig … Wo ist die Tür?

<Babette lacht, während sie die Tür öffnet. Darius hat das Haus betreten. Ein paar Minuten sind vergangen. Siehe! Der Geist erscheint>

**Darius:** Dort, ich kann den Geist sehen!

**Ghost:** My tea service, where's my tea service?

**Darius:** Your tea service?

**Ghost:** Who are you?

**Darius:** I'm Darius ...

**Ghost:** Babette! It was you who ran away screaming an hour ago ...

**Babette:** Of course! I've never seen a ghost before. So ... is it you, Grandpa?

**Ghost:** Yes, it's me ... I can't find my beloved tea service … I need it; otherwise, I can't rest in peace ...

**Darius:** I could try to find it with a spell!

<Darius is casting a spell>

**Darius:** Sorry, but I can't find it!

**Babette:** Ah, now I remember!

**Geist:** Mein Teeservice, wo ist mein Teeservice?

**Darius:** Dein Teeservice?

**Geist:** Wer bist du?

**Darius:** Ich bin Darius ...

**Geist:** Babette! Du warst es, die vor einer Stunde schreiend davon gelaufen ist ...

**Babette:** Natürlich! Ich habe noch nie zuvor einen Geist gesehen. Also ... bist du es, Opa?

**Geist:** Ja, ich bin es ... Ich kann mein geliebtes Teeservice nicht finden ... Ich brauche es; andernfalls kann ich nicht in Frieden ruhen ...

**Darius:** Ich könnte versuchen es mit einem Zauber zu finden!

<Darius ist dabei, einen Zauber zu sprechen>

**Darius:** Tut mir Leid, ich kann es nicht finden!

**Babette:** Ah, ich erinnere mich!

\<Babette knocked on a small stone in the wall, and then a few stones fell down. Now there's a small hollow space in the wall\>

**Babette:** Here's your tea service! I remembered that grandma always said that grandpa loved his tea service more than her. One day, I saw her hiding the tea service behind this wall.

**Ghost:** What?! I must talk with her about that immediately!

**Darius:** What about the tea services?

**Ghost:** Babette, please keep it and take care of it!

\<Babette is laughing\>

**Babette:** Thank you, Grandpa! I'll do so!

<Babette klopfte auf einen kleinen Stein in der Mauer und dann fielen ein paar Steine hinunter. Nun ist da ein kleiner Hohlraum in der Mauer>

**Babette:** Hier ist dein Teeservice! Ich habe mich erinnert, dass Oma immer sagte, dass Opa sein Teeservice mehr liebe als sie. Eines Tages sah ich sie das Teeservice hinter dieser Mauer verstecken.

**Geist:** Was?! Ich muss sofort mit ihr darüber sprechen!

**Darius:** Was ist mit dem Teeservice?

**Geist:** Babette, bitte behalte es und kümmere dich darum!

<Babette lacht>

**Babette:** Danke, Opa! Das werde ich tun!

# 9 Darius' Dream

<It's a stormy night in November. It's raining and thundering. Darius is dreaming ...>

**Darius:** You … you are Claudette!

<A cat-shaped silhouette is turning its head to Darius>

**Claudette:** Yes, I am Claudette.

**Darius:** Claudette! I haven't seen you since I finished my studies at the academy! I used to write you little letters. Unfortunately, there's never been an opportunity to meet you again and spend some time together ...

<Claudette is keeping quiet>

**Darius:** Can you hear me, Claudette?

**Claudette:** Darius, in one of your letters, you wrote that you loved me ... Why did you leave me? I was crying …
crying ...

**Darius:** Claudette, my master wouldn't have let me meet with you, you know that ...

# 9 Darius' Traum

<Es ist eine stürmische Nacht im November. Es regnet und donnert. Darius träumt ...>

**Darius:** Du ... du bist Claudette!

<Eine katzenförmige Silhouette dreht ihren Kopf zu Darius>

**Claudette:** Ja, ich bin Claudette.

**Darius:** Claudette! Ich habe dich, seit ich mein Studium an der Akademie beendete, nicht mehr gesehen! Ich schrieb dir damals Briefe. Unglücklicherweise gab es nie die Gelegenheit, dich wiederzutreffen und gemeinsam Zeit zu verbringen ...

<Claudette schweigt>

**Darius:** Kannst du mich hören, Claudette?

**Claudette:** Darius, in einem deiner Briefe schriebst du, du liebest mich ... Warum verließt du mich? Ich weinte ... weinte ...

**Darius:** Claudette, mein Meister hätte mich nicht mit dir treffen lassen – das weißt du ...

**Claudette:** No, Darius, you could have spent time with me, but you didn't … You left me alone! Now I'm dead, and there will be no more chance to come together!

<Darius is shocked>

**Darius:** Claudette, I love you ...

<Darius is starting to cry now>

**Darius:** This can't be true … You can't be dead! I would have heard that from somebody! Claudette! Claudette!

<Now Darius is waking up>

**Darius:** Claudette … I … I must try to find out where she is and if she's still alive ... But, now I should try to sleep a bit ...

<The next morning>

**Darius:** Oh dear, it was a strange night … Claudette ...

<Darius is sitting at the dining table in the dining room>

**Claudette:** Nein, Darius, du hättest Zeit mit mir verbringen können – hast du aber nicht … Du ließt mich allein! Nun bin ich tot und es wird keine Gelegenheit mehr geben, zusammenzukommen!

<Darius ist geschockt>

**Darius:** Claudette, ich liebe dich ...

<Darius fängt nun an zu weinen>

**Darius:** Das kann nicht wahr sein … Du kannst nicht tot sein! Das hätte ich von jemandem gehört! Claudette! Claudette!

<Jetzt wacht Darius auf>

**Darius:** Claudette … Ich … ich muss versuchen herauszufinden, wo sie ist und ob sie noch lebt … Aber nun sollte ich versuchen, etwas zu schlafen ...

<Am nächsten Morgen>

**Darius:** Oje, es ist eine seltsame Nacht gewesen … Claudette …

<Darius sitzt gerade am Esstisch im Esszimmer>

**Darius:** I'm wondering if it really was Claudette speaking to me in my dream … Or did my mind just played a trick on me? I don't know …

<Suddenly, an old book has fallen from the bookshelf>

**Darius:** Oh, why has it fallen down?

<Now Darius is approaching the book>

**Darius:** Ah, this is my old photo album … I can't believe it! A photo is lying next to it – a photo of Claudette …

**Darius:** Ich frage mich, ob es wirklich Claudette war, die in meinem Traum zu mir sprach … Oder hat mir einfach mein Gehirn einen Streich gespielt? Ich weiß es nicht …

<Plötzlich ist ein altes Buch vom Bücherregal gefallen>

**Darius:** Oh, warum ist es hinuntergefallen?

<Nun nähert sich Darius dem Buch>

**Darius:** Ah, das ist mein altes Fotoalbum … Ich kann es nicht glauben! Ein Foto liegt neben ihm – ein Foto von Claudette …

# 10 The Theft!

\<The summer festival has just begun, and Darius is casting some spells to entertain the people>

**Darius:** I love to use my magic for things like that. It's so nice that there haven't been any conflicts with any creatures lately.

\<Now a little boy is pulling on Darius' robe. Darius is laughing>

**Darius:** What's the matter, my friend?

**Little Boy:** You are so cool! I admire you! My sister admires you, too!

\<Darius is smiling>

**Darius:** I'm happy to hear that! I'm feeling honoured!

\<Darius doesn't notice that the little boy is taking his magic crystal>

**Darius:** Ah! Look, over there's your sister calling you!

# 10 Der Diebstahl!

\<Das Sommerfest hat gerade begonnen und Darius spricht gerade ein paar Zauber, um die Leute zu unterhalten\>

**Darius:** Ich liebe es, meine Magie für solche Dinge zu verwenden. Es ist so schön, dass es in letzter Zeit keinerlei Konflikte mit irgendwelchen Kreaturen gegeben hat.

\<Nun zieht ein kleiner Junge an Darius' Robe. Darius lacht\>

**Darius:** Was ist los, mein Freund?

**Kleiner Junge:** Du bist so cool! Ich bewundere dich! Meine Schwester bewundert dich auch!

\<Darius lächelt\>

**Darius:** Ich freue mich, das zu hören! Ich fühle mich geehrt!

\<Darius bemerkt nicht, dass der kleine Junge seinen magischen Kristall nimmt\>

**Darius:** Ah! Schau, dort vorne ruft deine Schwester nach dir!

&lt;The little boy is running to his sister, laughing&gt;

**Darius:** Those are nice kids! Well, I should continue to entertain the people ...

&lt;Behold! Darius notices that his crystal is gone&gt;

**Darius:** Where's my crystal? Could the little boy have stolen it? Where are the two children?!

&lt;Now Derek is coming to Darius&gt;

**Derek:** Darius, you should have a look at that!

**Darius:** What do you mean?

**Derek:** There are two kids who are summoning pretty fairies by using a crystal!

**Darius:** Pardon? That's my magic crystal! The little boy must have stolen it! Please lead me to them!

**Derek:** Of course!

&lt;Darius and Derek are on the marketplace, where the two kids are using Darius' crystal&gt;

<Der kleine Junge rennt lachend zu seiner Schwester>

**Darius:** Das sind nette Kinder! Nun, ich sollte weitermachen, die Leute zu unterhalten ...

<Siehe! Darius bemerkt, dass sein Kristall fort ist>

**Darius:** Wo ist mein Kristall? Könnte ihn der kleine Junge gestohlen haben? Wo sind die beiden Kinder?!

<Nun kommt Derek zu Darius>

**Derek:** Darius, du solltest dir das mal ansehen!

**Darius:** Was meinst du?

**Derek:** Da sind zwei Kinder, die hübsche Feen mit einem Kristall beschwören!

**Darius:** Wie bitte? Das ist mein magischer Kristall! Der kleine Junge muss ihn gestohlen haben! Bitte führe mich zu ihnen!

**Derek:** Natürlich!

<Darius und Derek sind auf dem Marktplatz, wo die zwei Kinder Darius' Kristall benutzen>

**Darius:** Stop that, please!

<The people are staring at him>

**Darius:** You both know that this is MY crystal!

<Now the little boy is crying>

**Little Boy:** I'm so sorry … It's true. I stole it a few minutes ago …

**Darius:** No problem, please give it back to me.

**Little Boy:** Sure, here you are!

**Darius:** Thank you, but never do that again, ok?

**Little Boy:** I swear that I'll never do that again!

<Darius is smiling>

**Darius:** Hört bitte damit auf!

<Die Leute starren ihn an>

**Darius:** Ihr beide wisst, dass das MEIN Kristall ist!

<Jetzt weint der kleine Junge>

**Kleiner Junge:** Es tut mir so Leid … Es ist wahr. Ich habe ihn vor ein paar Minuten gestohlen ...

**Darius:** Kein Problem, bitte gib ihn mir zurück.

**Kleiner Junge:** Sicher, hier!

**Darius:** Danke, aber bitte tue das nie wieder, ok?

**Kleiner Junge:** Ich schwöre, dass ich das nie wieder tun werde!

<Darius lächelt>

# 11 A feast for the Queen!

<It's a sunny day in August. Darius, Derek, and some of the townspeople are preparing a feast for the Queen. They're very busy at the moment>

**Darius:** We should hang up some colourful balloons.

**Derek:** Yes, I know that she loves them very much! I think some of my recently cultivated, tall flowers, that smell so wonderful … I love flowers ...

**Darius:** Derek, you're wandering off the subject ...

**Derek:** Hm, what?! Oh, yes, you're right, sorry! Well, I think we should decorate the marketplace with my flowers.

**Darius:** Sure, that sounds nice!

<A few hours have passed. The whole marketplace is beautifully decorated, and all the townspeople are waiting for the Queen to come>

**Derek:** I'm so excited! I hope that she'll enjoy the feast!

# 11 Ein Fest für die Königin!

\<Es ist ein sonniger Tag im August. Darius, Derek und ein paar der Stadtbewohner bereiten gerade ein Fest für die Königin vor. Sie sind momentan sehr beschäftigt>

**Darius:** Wir sollten ein paar bunte Luftballons aufhängen.

**Derek:** Ja, ich weiß, dass sie sie sehr mag! Ich denke ein paar meiner kürzlich gezüchteten, großen Blumen, die so wundervoll riechen … Ich liebe Blumen ...

**Darius:** Derek, du schweifst vom Thema ab ...

**Derek:** Hm, was?! Oh, ja, du hast recht, Entschuldigung! Nun, ich denke, wir sollten den Marktplatz mit meinen Blumen dekorieren.

**Darius:** Sicher, das hört sich gut an!

\<Ein paar Stunden sind vergangen. Der ganze Marktplatz ist schön dekoriert und alle Stadtbewohner warten nun darauf, dass die Königin kommt>

**Derek:** Ich bin so aufgeregt! Ich hoffe, dass ihr das Fest gefallen wird!

**Darius:** Well, we've done our best ...

**Derek:** That's right!

**Darius:** Over there's the Queen. Wow, she looks so beautiful as always ... She reminds me of … Claudette ...

**Derek:** Welcome to our feast!

**Queen:** I'm so happy! Everything looks wonderful! I say thank you to all of you! This feast is not just for me, but for all of us! Let's celebrate and enjoy ourselves!

<Now the Queen is looking at Darius>

**Queen:** Darius, I'd like to dance with you!

<Darius is confused>

**Darius:** Sure, Your Majesty!

<Now the Queen and Darius are dancing and laughing>

**Queen:** Darius, you are a pretty good dancer.

<Darius is blushing>

**Darius:** Nun, wir haben unser Bestes gegeben ...

**Derek:** Das ist richtig!

**Darius:** Dort vorne ist die Königin. Wow, sie sieht so schön wie immer aus ... Sie erinnert mich an … Claudette ...

**Derek:** Willkommen zu unserem Fest!

**Königin:** Ich bin so glücklich! Alles sieht wundervoll aus! Ich bedanke mich bei euch allen! Dieses Fest ist nicht nur für mich, sondern für uns alle! Lasst uns tanzen und Spaß haben!

<Nun sieht die Königin zu Darius>

**Königin:** Darius, ich möchte mit dir tanzen!

<Darius ist verdutzt>

**Darius:** Sicher, Eure Majestät!

<Nun tanzen und lachen die Königin und Darius>

**Königin:** Darius, du bist ein ziemlich guter Tänzer.

<Darius errötet>

**Darius:** Thank you, Your Majesty! I'm glad that my dancing skills delight you. I don't dance very often …

<The Queen is laughing>

**Queen:** I heard that special potions, which can be made with alchemy, can cause a firework if mixed together …

**Darius:** Yes, that's right! If you like, I can make some immediately …

<The Queen is happy>

**Queen:** That would be so nice, Darius!

<Darius has just made the special potions>

**Darius:** Is everybody ready for a beautiful firework?

**Everybody:** YES!

<A beautiful firework's just started>

**Darius:** Danke, Eure Majestät! Ich bin froh, dass Euch meine Tanzfähigkeiten erfreuen. Ich tanze nicht sehr oft …

<Die Königin lacht>

**Königin:** Ich habe gehört, dass spezielle Tränke, die man mit Alchemie herstellen kann, ein Feuerwerk verursachen können, wenn sie zusammengemischt werden …

**Darius:** Ja, das ist richtig! Wenn Ihr möchtet, kann ich gleich welche herstellen …

<Die Königin ist glücklich>

**Königin:** Das wäre so schön, Darius!

<Darius hat gerade die speziellen Tränke hergestellt>

**Darius:** Ist jedermann bereit für ein schönes Feuerwerk?

**Jedermann:** JA!

<Ein schönes Feuerwerk hat gerade begonnen>

# 12 A Cold Winter's Day

<It's a cold day in December. It has been snowing pretty much since last week, and it still does. Darius is learning some new spells>

**Darius:** It's so cold today! If I hadn't a fireplace, I would die for sure.

<Darius is smiling while holding his warm teacup>

**Darius:** Hm ... Could it be that an ice dragon has come here and is causing this coldness? This would be a problem, and all the people living here wouldn't be safe anymore ...

<Darius is worried>

**Darius:** But I haven't heard its beautiful singing yet. Ice dragons can sing very well. Usually, they sing at midnight. So, because I haven't heard its singing yet, there shouldn't be an ice dragon around here.

<Darius is smiling>

**Darius:** These spells are pretty hard to learn. I think I've learned enough for today.

# 12 Ein kalter Wintertag

\<Es ist ein kalter Tag im Dezember. Es hat seit letzter Woche ziemlich viel geschneit und es schneit noch immer. Darius lernt gerade ein paar neue Zauber>

**Darius:** Es ist heute so kalt! Wenn ich keinen Kamin hätte, würde ich sicherlich sterben.

\<Darius lächelt, während er seine warme Teetasse hält>

**Darius:** Hm ... Könnte es sein, dass ein Eisdrache hierher gekommen ist und diese Kälte verursacht? Das wäre ein Problem, und all die Leute, die hier leben, wären nicht mehr sicher ...

\<Darius ist besorgt>

**Darius:** Aber ich habe seinen schönen Gesang noch nicht gehört. Eisdrachen können sehr gut singen. Gewöhnlich singen sie um Mitternacht. Also, da ich seinen Gesang nicht gehört habe, sollte es hier keinen Eisdrachen geben.

\<Darius lächelt>

**Darius:** Diese Zauber sind ziemlich schwierig zu erlernen. Ich denke, ich habe genug für heute gelernt.

I'm feeling like making a snowman ... Well, why not? I'll do that!

<Darius has just left his home, and now he's in his garden>

**Darius:** I've always enjoyed making snowmen since I was a little cat ...

<Darius is laughing>

**Darius:** Nobody is outside; they're all in their warm homes.

<Behold! Some imps are coming>

**Darius:** Greetings to you! I see, you'd like to give me a hand, right?

<The imps are jumping up and down now. Darius and the imps are making not only one but many snowmen. Some are tiny, some are big, some look friendly, and some look frightening>

**Darius:** That's fun, isn't it?

Ich bin in Stimmung, einen Schneemann zu bauen ... Nun, warum nicht, das tue ich!

<Darius hat gerade sein Zuhause verlassen und ist nun im Garten>

**Darius:** Mir hat es immer Spaß gemacht, Schneemänner zu bauen, seit ich eine kleine Katze war ...

<Darius lacht>

**Darius:** Niemand ist draußen; sie sind alle in ihren warmen Häusern.

<Siehe! Da kommen ein paar Kobolde>

**Darius:** Seid gegrüßt! Ich sehe, ihr möchtet mir helfen, richtig?

<Die Kobolde springen nun auf und ab. Darius und die Kobolde bauen nicht nur einen, sondern viele Schneemänner. Manche sind winzig, manche sind groß, manche sehen freundlich aus, manche sehen furchterregend aus>

**Darius:** Das macht Spaß, nicht wahr?

<The imps are laughing>

**Darius:** You know what? Let's go inside the house and have dinner together – how does that sound?

<The imps are jumping up and down while laughing. Now Darius and the imps are sitting at a small table and enjoying their meal>

\<Die Kobolde lachen\>

**Darius:** Wisst ihr was? Lasst uns ins Haus gehen und zusammen zu Abend essen – wie hört sich das an?

\<Die Kobolde springen auf und ab, während sie lachen. Nun sitzen Darius und die Kobolde an einem kleinen Tisch und genießen ihr Mahl\>

# 13 The Magic Bikini

<It's a hot day in July. Darius has just woken up>

**Darius:** Ah, it's a beautiful day! I feel as if I were ten years younger!

<Darius is smiling>

**Darius:** Well, I have to pay the Queen a visit today. I wonder why she asked me to come …

<Now Darius is stretching himself>

**Darius:** Ok, time to wash myself!

<Darius is having a shower>

**Darius:** Oh no! I forgot to buy something for breakfast!

<Suddenly, somebody has knocked on the door>

**Darius:** One moment, please!

<Darius has just opened the door>

# 13 Der magische Bikini

&lt;Es ist ein heißer Tag im Juli. Darius ist gerade aufgewacht&gt;

**Darius:** Ah, es ist ein schöner Tag! Ich fühle mich, als wäre ich zehn Jahre jünger!

&lt;Darius lächelt&gt;

**Darius:** Nun, ich muss heute der Königin einen Besuch abstatten. Ich frage mich, warum sie mich gebeten hat, zu kommen …

&lt;Nun streckt sich Darius&gt;

**Darius:** Ok, Zeit, mich zu waschen!

&lt;Darius duscht&gt;

**Darius:** Oh nein! Ich habe vergessen, etwas zum Frühstück zu kaufen!

&lt;Plötzlich hat jemand an die Tür geklopft&gt;

**Darius:** Einen Moment, bitte!

&lt;Darius hat gerade die Tür geöffnet&gt;

**Derek:** Good morning, Darius!

**Darius:** Good morning, Derek!

**Derek:** Here, this is for you!

<Derek has given Darius a little bag>

**Derek:** Delicious sandwiches!

**Darius:** Thank you so much! What a coincidence! I haven't had anything to eat until now because I had forgotten to buy something.

<Derek is laughing>

**Derek:** That's typical of you!

<Now Darius is in the Queen's palace. The Queen herself asked him to come>

**Darius:** Here I am, Your Majesty. What would you like to tell me?

**Queen:** Everyone but Darius shall leave now.

**Derek:** Guten Morgen, Darius!

**Darius:** Guten Morgen, Derek!

**Derek:** Hier, das ist für dich!

&lt;Derek hat Darius eine kleine Tüte gegeben&gt;

**Derek:** Köstliche Sandwiches!

**Darius:** Ich danke dir so sehr! Was für ein Zufall! Ich habe bis jetzt nichts zum Essen gehabt, weil ich vergessen hatte, etwas zu kaufen.

&lt;Derek lacht&gt;

**Derek:** Das ist typisch für dich!

&lt;Nun ist Darius im Palast der Königin. Die Königin selbst bat darum, dass er kommt&gt;

**Darius:** Hier bin ich, Eure Majestät. Was möchtet Ihr mir sagen?

**Königin:** Jeder außer Darius soll nun fortgehen.

<All guards and the Queen's lady-in-waiting are leaving. Now the Queen is speaking with her voice lowered ...>

**Queen:** Darius, please go to the village 'Titi-Si-Lilly' – do you know where that is?

**Darius:** Yes, of course. The best bikinis, made of the finest materials, can be bought there, and ...

**Queen:** Hush! Please don't speak so loudly ...

**Darius:** I'm sorry, Your Majesty.

**Queen:** So, as I said, please go to Titi-Si-Lilly and get me my bikini.

**Darius:** I'll do that right now. I'm leaving now, Your Majesty.

<Three hours have passed. Darius has arrived in Titi-Si-Lilly>

**Darius:** A beautiful village! I haven't been here for a long time ... Well, over there's the famous bikini-shop.

<In the shop>

<Alle Wachmänner und der Königin Zofe gehen fort. Nun spricht die Königin mit gesenkter Stimme ...>

**Königin:** Darius, bitte gehe in das Dorf „Titi-Si-Lilly" – weißt du wo es ist?

**Darius:** Ja, natürlich. Die besten Bikinis, gemacht aus den edelsten Materialien, kann man dort kaufen und ...

**Königin:** Sch! Bitte sprich nicht so laut ...

**Darius:** Entschuldigung, Eure Majestät.

**Königin:** Also, wie ich gesagt habe, bitte gehe nach Titi-Si-Lilly und hole mir meinen Bikini.

**Darius:** Ich werde das jetzt gleich tun. Ich breche nun auf, Eure Majestät.

<Drei Stunden sind vergangen. Darius ist in Titi-Si-Lilly angekommen>

**Darius:** Ein schönes Dorf! Ich bin lange Zeit nicht hier gewesen ... Nun, dort drüben ist das berühmte Bikinigeschäft.

<Im Geschäft>

**Merchant:** Ah, a new customer! Welcome to my shop! Can I help you?

<Darius is speaking with his voice lowered now>

**Darius:** I'm here to collect the Queen's bikini ...

<The merchant is laughing>

**Merchant:** Why are you speaking so quietly? My bikinis are famous all over the world!

**Darius:** Well, I think that the Queen feels a bit embarrassed ...

**Merchant:** Ah, there's no reason for that! Here you are, the Queen's wonderful bikini!

**Darius:** Thank you! Goodbye!

<Three and a half hours later ...>

**Darius:** Here's your 'Titi-Si-Lilly-Bikini', Your Majesty.

**Queen:** Thank you so much, Darius!

**Händler:** Ah, ein neuer Kunde! Willkommen in meinem Geschäft! Was wünschst du?

&lt;Darius spricht nun mit gesenkter Stimme&gt;

**Darius:** Ich bin hier, um der Königin Bikini abzuholen ...

&lt;Der Händler lacht&gt;

**Händler:** Warum sprichst du so leise? Meine Bikinis sind auf der ganzen Welt berühmt!

**Darius:** Nun, ich denke, dass es der Königin etwas peinlich ist ...

**Händler:** Ah, es gibt keinen Grund dazu! Hier, der Königin wundervoller Bikini!

**Darius:** Danke! Auf Wiedersehen!

&lt;Dreieinhalb Stunden später ...&gt;

**Darius:** Hier ist Euer „Titi-Si-Lilly-Bikini", Eure Majestät.

**Königin:** Ich danke dir so sehr, Darius!

# 14 The Ritual of the Orcs

<It's a foggy night in November. Darius has fallen asleep in his chair. Loud chanting can be heard>

**Babette:** Oh dear, what's that noise?

<Babette is looking out of the window>

**Babette:** That's strange … There is a tall flame in the middle of the forest! But, the trees aren't burning ... I'd better go to Darius and tell him that!

<Now Babette is standing in front of Darius' house>

**Babette:** Darius! Please open the door!

<Darius is slowly waking up>

**Darius:** Babette?! Sure, please wait a moment!

<Darius has just opened the door>

**Babette:** Darius, there's a tall flame in the forest! Hush … Do you hear that noise?

# 14 Das Ritual der Orks

&lt;Es ist eine neblige Nacht im November. Darius ist auf seinem Stuhl eingeschlafen. Man kann lauten Gesang hören&gt;

**Babette:** Oje, was ist das für ein Lärm?

&lt;Babette schaut gerade zum Fenster hinaus&gt;

**Babette:** Das ist seltsam … Dort ist eine große Flamme inmitten des Waldes! Aber die Bäume brennen nicht ... Ich sollte besser zu Darius gehen und ihm das sagen!

&lt;Nun steht Babette vor Darius' Hause&gt;

**Babette:** Darius! Bitte öffne die Tür!

&lt;Darius wacht langsam auf&gt;

**Darius:** Babette?! Sicher, bitte warte einen Moment!

&lt;Darius hat soeben die Tür geöffnet&gt;

**Babette:** Darius, da ist eine große Flamme im Wald! Sch … Hörst du diesen Lärm?

**Darius:** Those are voices of orcs … Oh dear, they are performing a ritual!

**Babette:** We must stop them!

<Now Darius and Babette are running into the forest>

**Darius:** Oh no, they are trying to summon a demon!

**Babette:** A demon?!

**Darius:** Yes, please stay here! It's too dangerous for you!

**Babette:** No, I'll beat them up with my trunk!

<Behold! Babette is running to the orcs>

**Darius:** Oh dear ...

<Babette is beating them up. Some of the orcs are running away screaming, while others are climbing up a tree. Babette is laughing>

**Darius:** I think the ritual is interrupted now. I can seal the gate to hell now!

**Darius:** Das sind Stimmen von Orks … Oje, sie halten ein Ritual ab!

**Babette:** Wir müssen sie aufhalten!

<Nun rennen Darius und Babette in den Wald>

**Darius:** Oh nein, sie versuchen, einen Dämon zu beschwören!

**Babette:** Einen Dämon?!

**Darius:** Ja, bitte bleibe hier! Es ist zu gefährlich für dich!

**Babette:** Nein, ich werde sie mit meinem Rüssel vermöbeln!

<Siehe! Babette rennt zu den Orks>

**Darius:** Oje ...

<Babette vermöbelt sie. Manche der Orks rennen schreiend davon, während andere einen Baum hinaufklettern. Babette lacht>

**Darius:** Ich glaube, das Ritual ist nun unterbrochen. Ich kann nun das Tor zur Hölle versiegeln!

**Babette:** All right!

<Now Darius is casting a spell to seal the gate to hell. A few minutes have passed. The gate has disappeared>

**Babette:** We did it!

**Darius:** Yes, thank you very much for your help!

**Babette:** Alles klar!

<Nun spricht Darius einen Zauber, um das Tor zur Hölle zu versiegeln. Ein paar Minuten später. Das Tor ist verschwunden>

**Babette:** Wir haben es geschafft!

**Darius:** Ja, ich danke dir sehr für deine Hilfe!

# 15 The Escort

**Queen:** Darius, please escort my dear sister. She should be in 'Sparkling-Waterfall-Village' at the moment. I know that because I received a letter from her yesterday. There should also be her lady-in-waiting.

**Darius:** I'll bring them unscathed to you, Your Majesty!

**Queen:** I know that I can rely on you, my dear Darius!

\<Darius is blushing\>

**Darius:** T-thank you, Your Majesty. I'm leaving now.

\<Darius is traveling through forests and over hills now. Five hours have passed. He's finally arrived in Sparkling-Waterfall-Village\>

**Darius:** Oh dear, it has been more tiring than I thought ... Over there is an inn. I'll get myself something to eat and ask the publican where I can find the Queen's sister.

\<Now Darius is eating a delicious meal while asking the publican ...\>

# 15 Die Eskorte

**Königin:** Darius, bitte eskortiere meine liebe Schwester. Sie sollte im Moment in „Sparkling-Waterfall-Village" sein. Ich weiß das, weil ich gestern einen Brief von ihr erhalten habe. Dort sollte auch ihre Zofe sein.

**Darius:** Ich bringe sie unversehrt zu Euch, Eure Majestät!

**Königin:** Ich weiß, dass ich mich auf dich verlassen kann, mein lieber Darius!

<Darius wird rot>

**Darius:** D-danke, Eure Majestät. Ich breche nun auf.

<Darius reist nun durch Wälder und über Hügel. Fünf Stunden sind vergangen. Er ist endlich in Sparkling-Waterfall-Village angekommen>

**Darius:** Oje, es ist anstrengender gewesen, als ich dachte ... Da vorne ist ein Gasthaus. Ich werde mir etwas zu essen holen und den Schankwirt fragen, wo ich der Königin Schwester finden kann.

<Nun isst Darius ein köstliches Mahl, während er den Schankwirt fragt ...>

**Darius:** I'm looking for the Queen's sister and her lady-in-waiting. Do you know where they are at the moment?

**Publican:** Ah, sure! They arrived yesterday in the evening. I saw them near the bridge.

**Darius:** Thank you so much!

&lt;After Darius had eaten, he's gone to the bridge&gt;

**Darius:** Hm, I can't see them … Wait – I can hear a female voice crying … Ah, over there!

&lt;Darius is running into an abandoned hut now&gt;

**Darius:** Is there somebody?

&lt;A man is shouting …&gt;

**A Man:** Get lost, you fool!

**Darius:** Who are you? What are you doing?

**A Man:** I've tied up the Queen's dear sister and her lady-in-waiting!

**Darius:** Ich suche nach der Königin Schwester und ihrer Zofe. Weißt du wo sie im Moment sind?

**Schankwirt:** Ah, sicher! Sie kamen gestern Abend hier an. Ich habe sie in der Nähe der Brücke gesehen.

**Darius:** Ich danke dir sehr!

<Nachdem Darius gegessen hatte, ist er zur Brücke gegangen>

**Darius:** Hm, ich kann sie nicht sehen … Warte – ich kann eine weibliche Stimme weinen hören … Ah, dort vorne!

<Darius rennt nun in eine verlassene Hütte>

**Darius:** Ist hier jemand?

<Ein Mann schreit ...>

**Ein Mann:** Verzieh dich, du Narr!

**Darius:** Wer bist du? Was machst du?

**Ein Mann:** Ich habe der Königin geliebte Schwester und ihre Zofe gefesselt!

**A Man:** I've also taken all of their money!

**Darius:** Let them free immediately, or I'll turn you into ash!

**A Man:** Try to defeat me!

<Darius to himself ...>

**Darius:** Where is he? It is so dark in here ...

<Darius has cast a spell. Now the inside of the hut is well lit>

**Darius:** Ah, there you are!

<Behold! The man is running away>

**Darius:** You little ... Oh, there you are!

<Now Darius is cutting the bonds>

**Sister of the Queen:** Thank you so much for rescuing us, Darius!

**Darius:** There's no need to thank me, milady. I'm going to escort both of you to the Queen.

**Ein Mann:** Ich habe auch all ihr Geld genommen!

**Darius:** Lass sie sofort frei, oder ich werde dich in Asche verwandeln!

**Ein Mann:** Versuche mich zu besiegen!

<Darius zu sich selbst ...>

**Darius:** Wo ist er? Es ist hier so dunkel ...

<Darius hat einen Zauber gesprochen. Nun ist das Innere der Hütte gut beleuchtet>

**Darius:** Ah, dort bist du!

<Siehe! Der Mann rennt davon>

**Darius:** Du kleiner ... Oh, dort seid Ihr!

<Nun schneidet Darius die Fesseln durch>

**Der Königin Schwester:** Ich danke dir so sehr, dass du uns gerettet hast, Darius!

**Darius:** Es gibt keinen Grund, mir zu danken, Milady. Ich werde Euch beide zur Königin eskortieren.

**Sister of the Queen:** Thank you!

**Der Königin Schwester:** Danke!

# 16 The Kidnapped Daughter

\<Darius is mixing a few potions. It's warm and sunny outside – just a beautiful day in August. Now Darius is hearing a loud scream and the beats of a dragon's wings. Darius has just run to a window to see what is happening\>

**Darius:** A dragon has captured a girl! I must rescue her … Where could the dragon live? Hm … I know, on the mountain in the 'Emerald Waterfall Valley'. I'd better go there right away!

\<Now Darius is running as fast as he can to the Emerald Waterfall Valley\>

**Darius:** As I expected! The dragon is flying up to the mountain. I should use a levitation spell to get there!

\<Darius has just cast the spell, and now he's flying in the air\>

**Darius:** I'll be there very shortly!

\<Darius has reached the peak of the mountain\>

# 16 Die entführte Tochter

&lt;Darius mischt gerade ein paar Tränke. Es ist warm und sonnig draußen – einfach ein schöner Tag im August. Nun hört Darius einen lauten Schrei und das Schlagen der Flügel eines Drachen. Darius ist gerade zu einem Fenster gerannt, um zu sehen, was geschieht&gt;

**Darius:** Ein Drache hat ein Mädchen geschnappt! Ich muss sie retten … Wo könnte der Drache leben? Hm … Ich weiß, auf dem Berg im „Emerald Waterfall Valley". Ich sollte besser jetzt gleich dort hingehen!

&lt;Nun rennt Darius so schnell er kann zum Emerald Waterfall Valley&gt;

**Darius:** Wie ich erwartet habe! Der Drache fliegt zum Berg hinauf. Ich sollte einen Schwebezauber verwenden, um dorthin zu gelangen!

&lt;Darius hat gerade den Zauber gesprochen und nun fliegt er durch die Luft&gt;

**Darius:** Ich werde in Kürze da sein!

&lt;Darius hat den Gipfel des Berges erreicht&gt;

**Darius:** Are you all right?

**Girl:** Yes, I'm fine, thanks! Why are you here?

**Darius:** I've come here as soon as I could to rescue you!

<The girl is laughing now>

**Girl:** I don't need to be rescued! I love living here! The dragon is my friend now! He's so kind!

**Darius:** Why were you screaming after he had captured you if he's so kind?

**Girl:** I just said, 'The dragon is my friend NOW.' I didn't know that he was kind then!

**Darius:** Well, alright. If you are fine with it … But, what should I tell your parents? Who are your parents, by the way?

<The girl is smiling>

**Darius:** Bist du in Ordnung?

**Mädchen:** Ja, ich bin in Ordnung, danke! Warum bist du hier?

**Darius:** Ich bin, so schnell ich konnte, hier hergekommen, um dich zu retten!

&lt;Das Mädchen lacht nun&gt;

**Mädchen:** Ich brauche nicht gerettet zu werden! Ich liebe es, hier zu leben! Der Drache ist nun mein Freund! Er ist so nett!

**Darius:** Warum hast du dann geschrien, nachdem er dich geschnappt hatte, wenn er so nett ist?

**Mädchen:** Ich habe gerade gesagt: „Der Drache ist NUN mein Freund." Ich wusste zu jener Zeit nicht, dass er nett ist!

**Darius:** Nun, alles klar. Wenn es dir gefällt … Aber, was soll ich deinen Eltern sagen? Wer sind eigentlich deine Eltern?

&lt;Das Mädchen lächelt&gt;

**Girl:** My parents are Antonius Laudis and Lina Tertia Laudis.

**Darius:** Oh, you are the daughter of the Laudis family! Your family is very rich!

**Girl:** Yes, my family is also very boring! Please tell them that I'd like to live here. But I'll visit mum and dad every time I feel like doing that.

**Darius:** Ok, I'll do so. Goodbye!

**Girl:** Bye-bye!

**Mädchen:** Meine Eltern sind Antonius Laudis und Lina Tertia Laudis.

**Darius:** Oh, du bist die Tochter der Laudis Familie! Deine Familie ist sehr reich!

**Mädchen:** Ja, meine Familie ist auch sehr langweilig! Bitte sage ihnen, dass ich hier leben möchte. Aber ich werde Mama und Papa jedes Mal besuchen, wenn mir danach ist.

**Darius:** Ok, das werde ich tun. Auf Wiedersehen!

**Mädchen:** Tschüss!

# 17 A Stone From a Rainbow Sun I

<It's a warm night in summer. Darius is observing the stars while sitting on the beach. Now he is seeing a small stone falling from the sky ...>

**Darius:** Wow, what's that?

<Now Darius is swimming to the area where the stone has just fallen in>

**Darius:** There, it is underneath me! I need to dive ...

<Darius has just taken the stone>

**Darius:** Wow, what a beautiful stone! It's shining in different colours … like a rainbow! I want to examine it in my laboratory!

<Darius has just entered his laboratory>

**Darius:** So ...

<Darius has just put the stone in a metal device. Now he is doing some experiments. Six hours later ...>

# 17 Ein Stein
## von einer Regenbogensonne I

<Es ist eine warme Nacht im Sommer. Darius beobachtet gerade die Sterne, während er am Strand sitzt. Nun sieht er einen kleinen Stein vom Himmel fallen ...>

**Darius:** Wow, was ist das?

<Nun schwimmt Darius zu dem Bereich, wo gerade der Stein hineingefallen ist>

**Darius:** Dort, er ist unter mir! Ich muss tauchen ...

<Darius hat soeben den Stein genommen>

**Darius:** Wow, was für ein schöner Stein! Er scheint in verschiedenen Farben … wie ein Regenbogen! Ich will ihn in meinem Labor untersuchen!

<Darius hat gerade sein Labor betreten>

**Darius:** So ...

<Darius hat gerade den Stein in eine metallene Vorrichtung gelegt. Nun macht er ein paar Experimente. Sechs Stunden später ...>

**Darius:** I'm fascinated! This stone has mighty magic power! This stone mustn't fall into the wrong hands! I'd better keep it in my specially sealed cellar ...

<After Darius had brought the stone to a safe place, he's gone to bed. Darius is sleeping now>

**Voice:** Darius … Darius … Please talk to me ...

**Darius:** Who are you?

**Voice:** I'm Salyna ...

**Darius:** Salyna? I don't know you.

**Salyna:** You know me; I'm the stone you found ...

**Darius:** How can you speak to me?

**Salyna:** I'm only able to speak to you while you're sleeping ... I'm from a so called 'rainbow sun'. Unfortunately, I fell from a rainbow bridge while I was playing with my friends ...

**Darius:** Ich bin fasziniert! Dieser Stein besitzt mächtige magische Kraft! Dieser Stein darf nicht in die falschen Hände geraten! Ich sollte ihn besser in meinem speziell versiegelten Keller aufbewahren ...

<Nachdem Darius den Stein an einen sicheren Ort gebracht hatte, ist er ins Bett gegangen. Darius schläft nun>

**Stimme:** Darius ... Darius ... Bitte sprich mit mir ...

**Darius:** Wer bist du?

**Stimme:** Ich bin Salyna ...

**Darius:** Salyna? Ich kenne dich nicht.

**Salyna:** Du kennst mich; ich bin der Stein, den du gefunden hast ...

**Darius:** Wie kannst du mit mir sprechen?

**Salyna:** Mir ist es nur möglich, mit dir zu sprechen, während du schläfst ... Ich bin von einer so genannten „Regenbogensonne". Unglücklicherweise fiel ich von einer Regenbogenbrücke, während ich mit meinen Freunden spielte ...

**Darius:** I see ...

**Salyna:** Darius?

**Darius:** Yes?

**Salyna:** Please try to send me back to the rainbow sun! I'm so sad ... I'm missing my friends ...

**Darius:** Sure ... I'll try my best! But how could I help you? How could I send you back? By casting a spell?

**Salyna:** There's an old ritual ... If you perform that, I can fly home ...

**Darius:** All right, then! Please tell me all the things I need to know!

<Now Salyna is explaining to Darius how to perform the ritual>

**Darius:** Verstehe ...

**Salyna:** Darius?

**Darius:** Ja?

**Salyna:** Bitte versuche, mich zurück zur Regenbogensonne zu schicken! Ich bin so traurig ... Ich vermisse meine Freunde ...

**Darius:** Sicher ... Ich werde mein Bestes versuchen! Aber wie könnte ich dir helfen? Wie könnte ich dich zurückschicken? Durch das Wirken eines Zaubers?

**Salyna:** Es gibt ein altes Ritual ... Wenn du das abhältst, kann ich nach Hause fliegen ...

**Darius:** Alles klar! Bitte sage mir alles, was ich wissen muss!

\<Nun erklärt Salyna Darius, wie man das Ritual abhält\>

# 18 A Stone From a Rainbow Sun II

<Darius is working in his laboratory ...>

**Darius:** Alright, I need some more ingredients for the potion, which I have to pour over Salyna … Eh, the stone … Yes. I need a piece of an orc's bone and a bit of a dragon's blood … Both ingredients aren't easy to get ... I know that an orc tribe was attacked by a dragon a month ago … Maybe I'll find what I need there?

<Now Darius is walking to the place where the orc tribe lived>

**Darius:** I should be there soon.

<A few minutes later ...>

**Darius:** Here it is … What a mess! Ah, over there's an orc's skeleton!

<Darius has just taken a piece of bone>

**Darius:** Alright … Well, where could I find some dragon's blood? I'm lucky!

# 18 Ein Stein
## von einer Regenbogensonne II

&lt;Darius arbeitet gerade in seinem Labor ...&gt;

**Darius:** Alles klar, ich brauche ein paar mehr Ingredienzen für den Trank, den ich über Salyna gießen muss ... Äh, den Stein ... Ja. Ich brauche ein Stück eines Ork-Knochen und ein bisschen Blut eines Drachen ... Beide Ingredienzen sind nicht leicht zu bekommen ... Ich weiß, dass vor einem Monat, ein Orkstamm von einem Drachen angegriffen wurde ... Vielleicht finde ich dort, was ich brauche?

&lt;Nun läuft Darius zu dem Ort, wo der Orkstamm lebte&gt;

**Darius:** Ich sollte bald da sein.

&lt;Ein paar Minuten später ...&gt;

**Darius:** Hier ist es ... Was für ein Chaos! Ah, dort ist ein Skelett eines Orks.

&lt;Darius hat gerade ein Stück vom Knochen genommen&gt;

**Darius:** Alles klar ... Nun, wo könnte ich etwas Drachenblut finden? Ich habe Glück!

Eh, sad for the dragon, but great for me! Over there's a dragon's leg!

<Now Darius is filling a bit of the blood from the leg into a little bottle>

**Darius:** Fantastic! Now I've got everything I need to make the potion for Salyna!

<Darius is back in his laboratory and mixing the potion>

**Darius:** Done! Everything that's left to do is wait until it's night and then pour this portion over the stone.

<A few hours later>

**Darius:** It's time now ...

<Darius is walking to the beach>

**Darius:** I wish you all the best, Salyna! Maybe we'll see each other again some day ...

<Darius is pouring the potion over the stone now. Behold! The stone is beginning to fly. A few minutes have passed. The stone is flying to the sky very fast>

Äh, traurig für den Drachen, aber großartig für mich! Dort drüben ist ein Bein eines Drachen!

<Nun füllt Darius etwas Blut von dem Bein in eine kleine Flasche>

**Darius:** Fantastisch! Nun habe ich alles, was ich brauche, um den Trank für Salyna zuzubereiten!

<Darius ist zurück in seinem Labor und mischt den Trank>

**Darius:** Fertig! Alles, was jetzt noch zu tun ist, ist zu warten, bis es Nacht ist, und dann diesen Trank über den Stein zu gießen.

<Ein paar Stunden später>

**Darius:** Nun ist es Zeit ...

<Darius läuft gerade zum Strand>

**Darius:** Ich wünsche dir alles Gute, Salyna! Vielleicht werden wir uns eines Tages wiedersehen ...

<Darius gießt nun den Trank über den Stein. Siehe! Der Stein beginnt zu fliegen. Ein paar Minuten sind vergangen. Der Stein fliegt sehr schnell gen Himmel>

**Darius:** Farewell!

<Darius has just gone to bed>

**Darius:** I'm a bit sad … But it's the best for her …

<Darius has fallen asleep>

**Salyna:** Darius?

**Darius:** Salyna? Are you ok?

**Salyna:** I'm fine! Thank you so much for everything you've done for me! I'm so happy to be back home again!

**Darius:** I'm so glad that I could help you!

**Salyna:** Darius?

**Darius:** Salyna?

**Salyna:** I know that you're sad. I'm no longer by your side … But, due to the potion, I'm able to talk to you now even though I'm so far away from you.

**Darius:** Leb wohl!

<Darius ist gerade ins Bett gegangen>

**Darius:** Ich bin ein bisschen traurig … Aber es ist das Beste für sie …

<Darius ist eingeschlafen>

**Salyna:** Darius?

**Darius:** Salyna? Bist du ok?

**Salyna:** Mir geht's gut! Ich danke dir so sehr für alles, was du für mich getan hast! Ich bin so glücklich, wieder zu Hause zu sein!

**Darius:** Ich bin so froh, dass ich dir helfen konnte!

**Salyna:** Darius?

**Darius:** Salyna?

**Salyna:** Ich weiß, dass du traurig bist. Ich bin nicht länger an deiner Seite … Aber, durch den Trank ist es mir nun möglich, mit dir zu sprechen, obwohl ich so weit weg von dir bin.

So, we can spend some time together when you're sleeping ...

**Darius:** I'm so happy to hear that, Salyna!

<Darius and Salyna are laughing>

Also, wir können Zeit miteinander verbringen, wenn du schläfst ...

**Darius:** Ich bin so glücklich, das zu hören, Salyna!

<Darius und Salyna lachen>

# 19 The Ill Lady-in-Waiting

&lt;The Queen asked Darius to heal her lady-in-waiting. She's been ill since last week, and her condition is getting worse ...&gt;

**Darius:** It seems that she was bitten by a 'Blood Shadow Bat'!

**Queen:** Oh dear ... Do you think you can help her?

**Darius:** Hm, there should be a spell ... If I remember correctly, my master said that there was a spell against this disease in his magic book, which he gave me so many years ago.

**Queen:** That's great! Where's the book?

**Darius:** It's in my cellar ... Please wait a moment ...

&lt;The book has appeared after Darius had cast a spell&gt;

**Queen:** That's awesome!

**Darius:** Thank you, Your Majesty.

# 19 Die kranke Zofe

<Die Königin hat Darius gebeten, ihre Zofe zu heilen. Sie ist seit letzter Woche krank und ihr Zustand verschlechtert sich ...>

**Darius:** Es scheint, dass sie von einer „Blut-Schatten-Fledermaus" gebissen worden ist!

**Königin:** Oje … Denkst du, du kannst ihr helfen?

**Darius:** Hm, es sollte einen Zauber geben ... Wenn ich mich recht erinnere, sagte mein Meister, dass es in seinem Zauberbuch, welches er mir vor vielen Jahren gegeben hat, einen Zauber gegen diese Krankheit gebe.

**Königin:** Das ist großartig! Wo ist das Buch?

**Darius:** Es ist in meinem Keller … Bitte wartet einen Moment ...

<Das Buch ist erschienen, nachdem Darius einen Zauber gesprochen hatte>

**Königin:** Das ist beeindruckend!

**Darius:** Danke, Eure Majestät.

<Now the lady-in-waiting is coughing and screaming>

**Darius:** Here is the spell! Wait … I also need the nectar of a special flower! Only casting the spell isn't enough …

**Queen:** A flower? Derek could help!

**Darius:** Yes, please let him be brought here!

**Queen:** Sure!

<A few minutes have passed. Derek has arrived>

**Derek:** What do you need, Darius?

**Darius:** Do you know where I could find a 'Bloody Bat Flower'?

<Derek is laughing>

**Darius:** Are you ok?

**Derek:** I've got one here! I had just picked some of them before I have been brought here. These flowers are so beautiful! I wanted to put them in a vase and …

<Nun hustet und schreit die Zofe>

**Darius:** Hier ist der Zauber! Wartet … Ich brauche auch den Nektar einer speziellen Blume! Nur den Zauber zu sprechen reicht nicht aus …

**Königin:** Eine Blume? Derek könnte helfen!

**Darius:** Ja, bitte lasst ihn hierher bringen!

**Königin:** Sicher!

<Ein paar Minuten sind vergangen. Derek ist angekommen>

**Derek:** Was brauchst du, Darius?

**Darius:** Weißt du, wo ich eine Blume namens „Blutige Fledermaus Blume" finden könnte?

<Derek lacht>

**Darius:** Bist du in Ordnung?

**Derek:** Ich habe eine hier! Ich hatte gerade ein paar davon gepflückt, bevor ich hierher gebracht worden bin. Diese Blumen sind so schön! Ich wollte sie in eine Vase tun und …

**Queen:** Please, give Darius the flower!

**Derek:** Oh … Yes … I'm sorry, Your Majesty! Here you are!

**Darius:** Thank you, Derek!

<While Darius is squeezing the flower, its nectar is dropping on the lady-in-waiting's forehead. Now Darius is casting the spell, and the lady-in-waiting is groaning ...>

**Queen:** Is it working, Darius?

**Derek:** Please don't interrupt him while he's casting the spell, Your Majesty.

**Queen:** Ah, please forgive me. I'm sorry.

<A few minutes later ... The lady-in-waiting is looking better now>

**Darius:** I've cured her!

**Queen:** Thank you so much, Darius!

**Königin:** Bitte gib Darius die Blume!

**Derek:** Oh … Ja … Es tut mir Leid, Eure Majestät! Hier!

**Darius:** Danke, Derek!

<Während Darius die Blume zerquetscht, tropft ihr Nektar auf die Stirn der Zofe. Nun spricht Darius den Zauber und die Zofe stöhnt ...>

**Königin:** Funktioniert es, Darius?

**Derek:** Bitte unterbrecht ihn nicht, während er den Zauber spricht, Eure Majestät.

**Königin:** Ah, bitte vergib mir. Es tut mir Leid.

<Ein paar Minuten später ... Die Zofe sieht besser aus>

**Darius:** Ich habe sie geheilt!

**Königin**: Ich danke dir so sehr, Darius!

# 20 An Unexpected Visit

\<It's a stormy day in October. Darius is reading a book about alchemy in his living room. Now somebody is knocking on the door ...\>

**Darius:** Oh, it seems that somebody has come to visit me. Who could it be?

\<Darius is opening the door now\>

**Quintus:** Darius!

**Darius:** Uncle Quintus! I haven't seen you for a long time! Please come in!

**Quintus:** Thank you!

\<Now Darius and Quintus are sitting in the living room. Darius is telling Quintus about his new experiments\>

**Quintus:** Oh, that's very interesting! I'm studying some texts of Saphira these days.

**Darius:** Saphira ... She's the wizard who finished the studies of magic with the highest marks possible, right?

# 20 Ein unerwarteter Besuch

<Es ist ein stürmischer Tag im Oktober. Darius liest gerade ein Buch über Alchemie in seinem Wohnzimmer. Nun klopft jemand an die Tür ...>

**Darius:** Oh, es scheint, dass jemand gekommen ist, um mich zu besuchen. Wer könnte es sein?

<Darius öffnet nun die Tür>

**Quintus:** Darius!

**Darius:** Onkel Quintus! Ich habe dich schon lange nicht mehr gesehen! Bitte komm herein!

**Quintus:** Danke!

<Jetzt sitzen Darius und Quintus im Wohnzimmer. Darius erzählt Quintus von seinen neuen Experimenten>

**Quintus:** Oh, das ist sehr interessant! Ich studiere ein paar Texte von Saphira dieser Tage.

**Darius:** Saphira … Sie ist die Zauberin, die das Studium der Magie mit den höchstmöglichen Noten abgeschlossen hat, richtig?

**Quintus:** So it is! She's amazing!

**Darius:** I agree! But why are you studying her texts? You are a historian and not a wizard, are you?

&lt;Quintus is smiling&gt;

**Quintus:** Of course I am, but she doesn't write only about magic but also about the HISTORY of magic.

**Darius:** That's interesting. Could you lend me the texts after you've read them?

**Quintus:** Yes, no problem. I'll send them to you very shortly.

**Darius:** Sounds nice!

**Quintus:** Well, it's late ... I should return home now.

**Darius:** I'm very happy that you've visited me, Quintus!

**Quintus:** It's been a beautiful day!

**Quintus:** So ist es! Sie ist beeindruckend!

**Darius:** Ich stimme zu! Aber warum studierst du ihre Texte? Du bist ein Historiker und kein Zauberer, nicht wahr?

&lt;Quintus lächelt&gt;

**Quintus:** Natürlich bin ich das, aber sie schreibt nicht nur über Magie, sondern auch über die GESCHICHTE der Magie.

**Darius:** Das ist interessant. Könntest du mir die Texte ausleihen, wenn du sie gelesen hast?

**Quintus:** Ja, kein Problem. Ich werde sie dir sehr bald zuschicken.

**Darius:** Hört sich gut an!

**Quintus:** Nun, es ist spät ... Ich sollte nun nach Hause zurückkehren.

**Darius:** Ich bin sehr glücklich, dass du mich besucht hast, Quintus!

**Quintus:** Es ist ein schöner Tag gewesen!

<Now Quintus is looking up at a tree which stands next to Darius' house>

**Quintus:** Eh, what's that up there?

**Darius:** What do you mean?

**Quintus:** That piece of cloth ...

<Darius has realized that it's the bikini top of the Queen and is blushing now>

**Darius:** Eh ... Well, that's the bikini top of the Queen, that I once collected for her ...

<Quintus is laughing>

**Quintus:** The Queen's bikini top? Well, that means that she may need it back as soon as possible ...

**Darius:** I'll teleport it to her immediately.

<Darius has cast a spell>

**Queen:** Oh dear, I'm partly naked ... Nobody must see me now ... That damn wind!

<Nun schaut Quintus zu einem Baum hinauf, der neben Darius' Haus steht>

**Quintus:** Äh, was ist das da oben?

**Darius:** Was meinst du?

**Quintus:** Jenes Stück Stoff da ...

<Darius hat erkannt, dass es das Bikinitop der Königin ist und errötet nun>

**Darius:** Äh ... Nun, das ist das Bikinitop der Königin, das ich einst für sie abgeholt habe ...

<Quintus lacht>

**Quintus:** Der Königin Bikinitop? Nun, das bedeutet, dass sie es wohl so schnell wie möglich zurück braucht ...

**Darius:** Ich werde es sofort zu ihr teleportieren.

<Darius hat einen Zauber gesprochen>

**Königin:** Oje, ich bin halbnackt ... Niemand darf mich jetzt sehen ... Dieser verdammte Wind!

&lt;Behold! The bikini top is lying next to her&gt;

**Queen:** Here it is! I'm so glad! If Darius teleported it?

&lt;Siehe! Das Bikinitop liegt neben ihr&gt;

**Königin:** Hier ist es! Ich bin so froh! Ob Darius es teleportiert hat?

# Übungen

## 1. Bilde das „Will-Future" in der richtigen Form von:
*to cast, to walk, to talk, to be, to draw, to celebrate, to love, to chase, to die, to kill*

1.1 I think Babette … a picture of Darius.

1.2 I … a spell to defeat the monster!

1.3 I think Derek … this flower!

1.4 Darius surely … there.

1.5 Maybe Darius and Quintus … along the river.

1.6 Salyna … to Darius in a few days.

1.7 We … a feast some day.

1.8 The leader of the orcs says that he … all the people of our town!

1.9 Sir Andrew … if you don't help him!

1.10 I ... this dragon!

## 2. Übersetze ins Deutsche

2.1 The Queen loves to go to the beach wearing her magic bikini.

2.2 Darius doesn't believe it is true that there aren't any dragons around here.

2.3 Derek spends most of his time with his flowers.

2.4 Don't be a fool! That would be too dangerous!

2.5 Quintus and Darius are laughing about the dancing imps.

2.6 I'm so tired today ... I don't feel like learning today.

2.7 Babette is having lunch with Darius at the moment.

2.8 Over there are orcs!

2.9 I'm exhausted … I need a cup of special tea!

2.10 Babette used to collect old paintings.

2.11 Derek has been working in his garden for ten hours now ...

2.12 Pass me the book, please!


**3. Bilde das „Past Perfect Progressive" in der 1.Person Plural**

3.1 to go

3.2 to live

3.3 to celebrate

3.4 to write

3.5 to hear

3.6 to talk

3.7 to answer

3.8 to listen

3.9 to swim

3.10 to run

3.11 to kill

3.12 to cast a spell

3.13 to protect

3.14 to save

3.15 to clean

3.16 to read

3.17 to make

3.18 to sleep

3.19 to shake

3.20 to fly

## 4. Übersetze ins Deutsche

4.1 When Darius left the house, he met Derek.

4.2 After Darius had learned a new spell, he tried to use it immediately.

4.3 The time I have spent with you has been beautiful.

4.4 Get out of here! Shadows are coming to slaughter us!

4.5 Please don't be silly; there must be a way out of here!

4.6 Derek, please give me a hand.

4.7 Don't you tell her about that!

4.8 What a rainy day! I won't go out now!

4.9 While Darius was studying, Derek was talking to his flowers.


## 5. Bringe die Sätze in die richtige Reihenfolge

5.1 Derek / fertilizing / his flowers. / is

5.2 in the lake. / often / Darius / swims

5.3 my / recently made / Where / robe? / is

5.4 Babette / a cake, / cleaned / ate / the floor / , and / left the house.

5.5 That's / potion! / dangerous / a

5.6 I / finished / in about / reading / two hours. / this book / will have

## 6. Übersetze ins Englische

6.1 Als Darius im Wald spazieren ging, begegnete er einem Troll.

6.2 Die Königin sagte, sie habe noch nie einen Drachen gesehen.

6.3 Wo ist mein linker Schuh? Ich kann ihn nirgends sehen ...

6.4 Der Händler fragte mich, ob ich wisse, wo das Gasthaus sei.

6.5 Sie ist heute gut gelaunt, also werde ich sie bitten, mir einen neuen Stuhl zu kaufen.

6.6 Die Sonne geht gerade auf und Darius frühstückt.

6.7 Darius hatte bereits drei Stunden in seinem Labor gearbeitet, als plötzlich Derek hineinkam.

6.8 Derek sagt, dass er zu dem Sommerfest gehen werde.

## 7. Bilde einen Relativsatz

7.1 Babette, (used to collect old paintings) , is walking over there.

7.2 Darius, (often talks with Salyna) , is going to stay there for three days.

7.3 Derek, (flowers I like) , is sitting on a bench in his garden.

7.4 The dragon, (is mighty) , usually flies over the forest at this time.

7.5 The tomcat (is lying in the hammock) over there often dreams of becoming rich.

7.6 My old friend, (I just saw), has become unfriendly.


## 8. Füge das passende Fragewort ein:
## why, who, how, when

8.1 ... did Babette visit her aunt?

- She visited her two weeks ago.

8.2 … don't you buy from that merchant?

- I don't think that he's trustworthy.

8.3 … do you communicate with Salyna?

- I communicate with her by sleeping.

8.4 … do you like the most?

- Me? Oh well, I like my flowers the most.

8.5 … did you learn your latest spell?
- That was two days ago.


## 9. Bilde einen Komparativsatz im „Simple Past"

9.1 Derek/be/good/at arranging flowers/Darius.

9.2 Quintus/know/much/about history/anybody else.

9.3 She/be/fast/Babette!

9.4 The Queen/dance/good/Darius.

9.5 Darius/work/often/in his laboratory/the other students.

9.6 Salyna/dream/often/about the earth/her friends.

9.7 Darius' master/be/good/all the other wizards.

9.8 The Queen/learn/how to paint/fast/her lady-in-waiting.

9.9 Babette/beat up/much/orcs/Darius.

9.10 Derek/be/clever/he looked.


## 10. Übersetze ins Deutsche

10.1 Derek and Babette were talking about Babette's home country in Derek's garden when it started to rain.

10.2 The Queen and Darius were having dinner when suddenly a herold needed to talk to her.

10.3 Derek is swimming in the lake, while a little imp is drinking orange juice.

10.4 Two little imps are arguing.

10.5 It had been snowing heavily when Derek arrived at Darius' house.

10.6 There's not even one potion left, so I'll have to make some new ones.

10.7 My friend should arrive in two days.

10.8 You should have taken more than one health potion with you!


## 11. Bilde das „Past Progressive" in der 3.Person Singular

11.1 to read

11.2 to say

11.3 to fight

11.4 to borrow

11.5 to lend

11.6 to collect

11.7 to play

11.8 to applaud

11.9 to water the flowers

11.10 to spend

11.11 to buy

11.12 to jump

11.13 to make an announcement

11.14 to punch

11.15 to press

11.16 to open

11.17 to smoke

11.18 to heal

11.19 to prepare

11.20 to strengthen

## 12. Bilde einen Superlativsatz im „Simple Past"

12.1 Darius/be/good!

12.2 Derek/cook/good!

12.3 Babette/collect/much!

12.4 The Queen/learn/a new language/fast!

12.5 The tomcat/eat/much!


## 13. Übersetze ins Deutsche

13.1 Darius has been listening to a singing bird for two hours now ...

13.2 Derek has been dreaming of growing the biggest flower on earth for many years.

13.3 Babette has been taking a shower since three o'clock, and she still hasn't left the bathroom yet!

13.4 Three imps have been going for a walk for ten hours now ...

13.5 The Queen has been playing the flute for many years.

13.6 Darius and Salyna have been laughing for half an hour now ...


## 14. Übersetze ins Englische

14.1 Sei gegrüßt, mein Freund!

14.2 Bitte hole mir den großen Kessel aus dem Keller!

14.3 Verlasse die Stadt sofort!

14.4 Mache dich bereit zu kämpfen!

14.5 Rege dich nicht auf!

14.6 Gute Nacht! Ich schließe meine Augen, wissend, dass ich mich nie wieder am Licht des Tages erfreuen kann.

14.7 Die Bäume hier im Wald sehen sehr furchteinflößend aus!

14.8 Die alte Frau war also eine Hexe?

14.9 Der Ältesten Bücher werden in dieser Bibliothek aufbewahrt.

14.10 Ich bin so froh, dass du mit mir zum Orkstamm gehst.

14.11 Dein Schwert ist mit schönen Edelsteinen verziert – wie teuer war es?

14.12 Diese Rüstung bietet besseren Schutz vor Magie, da Darius einen Zauber auf sie gewirkt hat!

14.13 Ich benötige dringend einen neuen Schild aus Stahl!

14.14 Mit dieser Armbrust kannst du nicht gegen den Drachen kämpfen!

14.15 Dieses Kettenhemd ist von hoher Qualität!

14.16 Das ist genau das Richtige für mich!

14.17 Der fremde Zauberer fragte Darius, ob er wisse, wie er heiße.

14.18 Eine schöne Frau, die sich selbst Julia nennt, ist heute zu Darius gekommen und hat ihn um einen Gefallen gebeten.

14.19 Derek und Babette feiern gerade eine Party.

14.20 Die Sonne geht gerade unter!

## 15. Übersetze ins Deutsche

15.1 Look! There are so many shooting stars in the sky!

15.2 This has been a beautiful day! Let's meet again next week, ok?

15.3 I swear that I just saw a ghost in the cellar!

15.4 Please believe me, I didn't steal that book!

15.5 Why are you screaming? That's just a tiny spider!

15.6 Never in my wildest dreams did I think that this could happen!

15.7 Ok, I'll take you to my lord.

15.8 Oh no! A thunderstorm! Go into your houses and stay there until the thunderstorm is gone!

15.9 Let him bring her to me! I'd like to hear what she's got to say myself.

15.10 He stood there without saying a word.


## 16. *Bilde das Adverb*

16.1 firm

16.2 excited

16.3 weak

16.4 fresh

16.5 strong

16.6 careless

16.7 offensive

16.8 loud

16.9 quiet

16.10 high

16.11 cruel

16.12 happy

16.13 extreme

16.14 warm

16.15 cold

16.16 glad

16.17 careful

16.18 sad

16.19 calm

16.20 bright

16.21 soft

## 17. Bilde das „Futur Progressive" in der 1.Person Singular

17.1 to talk

17.2 to play

17.3 to speak

17.4 to work

17.5 to write

17.6 to read

17.7 to catch

17.8 to bark

17.9 to teach

17.10 to travel

## 18. Bilde das „Simple Present" in der 3.Person Singular

18.1 to call

18.2 to bring

18.3 to lie

18.4 to love

18.5 to kiss

18.6 to dream

18.7 to reach

18.8 to burn

18.9 to heat up

18.10 to smile

## 19. Bringe die Sätze in die richtige Reihenfolge

19.1 Darius / against / a black dragon. / fought

19.2 When / Derek / his / flower? / first / get / did

19.3 Babette / a lot of / has to do / things / today.

19.4 How / this / potion / yellow / much / cost? / does

19.5 I'll / to the library. / the book / take

19.6 pretty / today. / noisy / in the / It is / marketplace

19.7 It's / this morning. / too cold / in the sea / to go swimming

19.8 Don't / me / disturb / , please!


## 20. Übersetze ins Deutsche

20.1 I really don't know what this spell is for.

20.2 Salyna has just met an old lady who she hadn't seen for a long time.

20.3 I'm sorry, but I do not know where she lives ...

20.4 The orcs and two dragons are attacking the castle!

20.5 Derek is brandishing his axe.

20.6 Darius isn't at home … That's strange!

20.7 You are not allowed to pass!

20.8 I never would have thought that I could purchase such a beautiful robe!

## 21. Übersetze ins Englische

21.1 Ein Fremder hat gestern die Stadt betreten und ist seitdem nicht mehr gesehen worden.

21.2 Ich muss etwas magischen Stoff kaufen, um eine neue Robe anzufertigen.

21.3 Es gibt keinen Grund zur Panik!

21.4 Genau so ist das! Gehe daher zu Darius!

21.5 Hilf uns! Unser Bauernhof brennt!

21.6 Wenn ich dich den Zauber gelehrt hätte, wärst du verschwunden!

21.7 Die Königin saß gestern auf einer Bank im Park, während sie ein Schokoeis aß.

21.8 Dieser Trank ist äußerst teuer – nein, ich will ihn nicht kaufen!

21.9 Dachtest du etwa, du könntest mich besiegen?!

21.10 Dein Großvater ging im Park spazieren und sprach mit den Vögeln, als wären es Menschen.

## 22. Übersetze ins Deutsche

22.1 Darius loves to take a bath late at night.

22.2 Babette's most favourite food is chocolate ice cream.

22.3 Derek and his wife were dancing in their garden at midnight.

22.4 Derek and Darius are on the way to a witch's house, which is located deep in the forest.

22.5 Darius and Babette have been swimming in the sea since five o'clock in the morning.

22.6 Darius has never slept in a dragon's refuge before.

22.7 This castle is very old; some people even say that sinister rituals were performed here.

22.8 I expect that you stand up early, have read these books by five o'clock, and go to sleep at eight o'clock.

22.9 Please, don't get me wrong … I just like you ...

22.10 Don't even try to do that! You'll regret it!

## 23. Übersetze ins Englische

23.1 Darius sagte, er habe heute Morgen die Königin besucht.

23.2 Derek bat Darius, ihn zu besuchen, sobald er seine Arbeit erledigt habe.

23.3 Derek und Babette fragten Darius, ob er wisse, wo man seltene Blumen finden könne.

23.4 Darius und Derek fragten den Fremden, wohin er gehen wolle.

23.5 Darius schlug vor, nicht mit den Orks einen Krieg anzufangen.

23.6 Die Königin schlug vor, neun Ritter zu dem verlassenen Anwesen zu schicken.

23.7 Darius dachte, er würde jene Nacht nicht überleben.

23.8 Darius und Derek dachten, die Königin würde sich nicht mit dem Anführer der Orks treffen.

23.9 Derek fragte seine Frau, ob sie ihm einen Krug mit kaltem Wasser bringen könne.

23.10 Darius sagte, er wäre nicht zu so später Stunde in den See gegangen.

## 24. Bilde den Komparativ

24.1 weak

24.2 strong

24.3 healthy

24.4 big

24.5 short

24.6 old

24.7 young

24.8 deep

24.9 high

24.10 clear

## 25. Bilde den Superlativ

25.1 stiff

25.2 tired

25.3 easy

25.4 hard

25.5 sunny

25.6 dark

25.7 bright

25.8 loud

25.9 elastic

25.10 clean

## 26.Bringe die Sätze in die richtige Reihenfolge

26.1 wizard / Darius / is / I know./ the best

26.2 seems / Babette/ to be / newly bought shoes./ with / her / pretty  satisfied

26.3  a black dragon / has never / seen / again. / Darius

26.4  in the abandoned castle / A necromancer / just a few minutes ago. / was seen

26.5 since / had been/ that morning. / watering / the beautiful flowers/ Derek

26.6 Mister Gnom's / Darius / can't stand / today./ behaviour

26.7  you / have/ my letter? / Dear Ms Babette, / received

26.8 into / for sure! / find / deeper / , and / you'll / the teasure / Go / the cave

26.9 touch / Don't / dare / my butt! / you

26.10 pretty / This / is/ creepy! / skeleton

**27.Setze das passende Wort ein:**
*a potion, helped, fertilizer, control, ghost, made, keep,*
*naked, mind, find, talked*

27.1 Derek has always … her wife whenever he could.

27.2 Darius has just … an awful smelling ...

27.3 Oh no! This creature is out of ...

27.4 Derek said that he wanted to buy a better … for his flowers.

27.5 Why are you afraid? A … is nothing to be afraid of!

27.6 My … is playing tricks on me.

27.7 I couldn't … my alchemy book!

27.8 Babette … to her best friend yesterday.

27.9 I heard that the Queen had been swimming … in the sea last Sunday!

27.10 Please … it – it's a present!

## 28. Setze das passende Fragewort ein:
## why, when, how, what, where

28.1 … did you fight against the ice dragon near Ilaferya Castle?

28.2 I asked him … he saw the group of orcs.

28.3 … about this kind of magic flower?

28.4  Of course, I wanted to know … happened!

28.5 … are you talking so loudly? Please calm down!

28.6 … was Babette wearing when she visited you?

28.7 … did you know that it was him?

28.8 I couldn't tell her … I've never sent her a letter.

28.9 I didn't know … Darius went.

28.10 … is the next eclipse of the sun?

### 29. Übersetze ins Deutsche

29.1 Darius was the first to invent this kind of potion.

29.2 It's amazing how fast these creatures can fly around!

29.3 Excuse me, could you show me the way to Sir Almond's mansion, please?

29.4 Sir Excellus would be reading a book about history when I saw him in the library.

29.5 No, magic is not the right thing, neither for a little girl nor a boy – it's too dangerous.

29.6 Alchemy is difficult to learn.

29.7 With this spell, I'm able to make snowflakes bigger!

29.8 Would you like to have a cool drink, Darius?

29.9 Supposing that there were no stars, how would you feel?

29.10 I wish I knew her name ...

## 30. Übersetze ins Englische

30.1 Sieh dir dieses Chaos an! Ein blöder Kobold hat mein ganzes Labor verwüstet!

30.2 Das glaube ich dir nicht! Du warst es, der die Toten erweckte und das Dorf zerstörte!

30.3 Mögest du einen Weg finden, das Böse aus dieser Halle zu vertreiben.

30.4 Der Traum war so real ... Ich frage mich, ob es tatsächlich nur ein Traum war ...

30.5 Möchtest du mit mir zur Festung der magischen Ritter gehen?

30.6 Kobolde mögen nicht besonders klug sein, aber sie sind sehr amüsant.

30.7 Ich werde dich die Kunst der Alchemie gelehrt haben, bevor ich sterbe.

30.8 Glaube an dein Herz!

30.9 Ich bin so glücklich, weil ich heute meinen ersten Zauber gelernt habe!

30.10 Du bist sehr tapfer! Ich glaube, ich hätte diesen Troll nicht in die Flucht schlagen können.

# Lösungsschlüssel

## 1. Übung

1.1 will draw

1.2 will cast

1.3 will love

1.4 will be

1.5 will walk

1.6 will talk

1.7 will celebrate

1.8 will kill

1.9 will die

1.10 will chase

## 2. Übung

2.1 Die Königin liebt es, ihren magischen Bikini tragend, an den Strand zu gehen.

2.2 Darius glaubt nicht, dass es wahr ist, dass es hier in der Umgebung keine Drachen gibt.

2.3 Derek verbringt den Großteil seiner Zeit mit seinen Blumen.

2.4 Sei kein Narr! Das wäre zu gefährlich!

2.5 Quintus und Darius lachen gerade über die tanzenden Kobolde.

2.6 Ich bin heute so müde ... Ich habe heute keine Lust zu lernen.

2.7 Babette isst gerade mit Darius zu Mittag.

2.8 Dort drüben sind Orks!

2.9 Ich bin erschöpft … Ich brauche eine Tasse Spezialtee!

2.10 Babette sammelte früher alte Gemälde.

2.11 Derek hat nun bereits zehn Stunden in seinem Garten gearbeitet ...

2.12 Bitte reiche mir das Buch!

## 3. *Übung*

3.1 We had been going

3.2 We had been living

3.3 We had been celebrating

3.4 We had been writing

3.5 We had been hearing

3.6 We had been talking

3.7 We had been answering

3.8 We had been listening

3.9 We had been swimming

3.10 We had been running

3.11 We had been killing

3.12 We had been casting a spell

3.13 We had been protecting

3.14 We had been saving

3.15 We had been cleaning

3.16 We had been reading

3.17 We had been making

3.18 We had been sleeping

3.19 We had been shaking

3.20 We had been flying

## 4. *Übung*

4.1 Als Darius das Haus verließ, traf er Derek.

4.2 Nachdem Darius einen neuen Zauber erlernt hatte, versuchte er ihn sofort zu verwenden.

4.3 Die Zeit, die ich mit dir verbracht habe, ist schön gewesen.

4.4 Verschwindet von hier! Schatten kommen, um uns abzuschlachten!

4.5 Bitte sei nicht albern; es muss einen Weg hier herausgeben!

4.6 Derek, bitte hilf mir.

4.7 Erzähl ihr nichts davon!

4.8 Was für ein verregneter Tag! Ich werde jetzt nicht nach draußen gehen!

4.9 Während Darius lernte, sprach Derek zu seinen Blumen.

## 5. Übung

5.1 Derek is fertilizing his flowers.

5.2 Darius often swims in the lake.

5.3 Where is my recently made robe?

5.4 Babette ate a cake, cleaned the floor, and left the house.

5.5 That's a dangerous potion!

5.6 I will have finished reading this book in about two hours.

## 6. Übung

6.1 When Darius was going for a walk in the forest, he met a troll.

6.2 The Queen said that she'd never seen a dragon.

6.3 Where's my left shoe? I can't see it anywhere ...

6.4 The merchant asked me if I knew where the inn was.

6.5 She's in a good mood today, so I'll ask her to buy me a new chair.

6.6 The sun is rising, and Darius is having breakfast.

6.7 Darius had been working in his laboratory for three hours when suddenly Derek came in.

6.8 Derek says that he's going to go to the summer festival.

## 7. Übung

7.1 Babette, who used to collect old paintings, is walking over there.

7.2 Darius, who often talks with Salyna, is going to stay there for three days.

7.3 Derek, whose flowers I like, is sitting on a bench in his garden.

7.4 The dragon, that/which is mighty, usually flies over the forest at this time.

7.5 The tomcat who is lying in the hammock over there often dreams of becoming rich.

7.6 My old friend, who I just saw, has become unfriendly.


## 8. Übung

8.1 when

8.2 why

8.3 how

8.4 who

8.5 when

## 9. *Übung*

9.1 Derek was better at arranging flowers than Darius.

9.2 Quintus knew more about history than anybody else.

9.3 She was faster than Berbette!

9.4 The Queen danced better than Darius.

9.5 Darius worked more often in his laboratory than the other students.

9.6 Salyna dreamed more often about the earth than her friends.

9.7 Darius' master was better than all the other wizards.

9.8 The Queen learned how to paint faster than her lady-in-waiting.

9.9 Babette beat up more orcs than Darius.

9.10 Derek was more clever/cleverer than he looked.


## 10. Übung

10.1 Derek und Babette unterhielten sich über Babettes Heimatland in Dereks Garten, als es zu regnen begann.

10.2 Die Königin und Darius aßen zu Abend, als plötzlich ein Bote mit ihr sprechen musste.

10.3 Derek schwimmt gerade im See, während ein kleiner Kobold Orangensaft trinkt.

10.4 Zwei kleine Kobolde streiten sich gerade.

10.5 Es hatte bereits stark geschneit, als Derek Darius' Haus erreichte.

10.6 Es ist nicht einmal ein Trank übrig, also werde ich ein paar neue machen müssen.

10.7 Mein Freund sollte in zwei Tagen ankommen.

10.8 Du hättest mehr als nur einen Heiltrank mitnehmen sollen!

## 11. Übung

11.1 He/She/It was reading

11.2 He/She/It was saying

11.3 He/She/It was fighting

11.4 He/She/It was borrowing

11.5 He/She/It was lending

11.6 He/She/It was collecting

11.7 He/She/It was playing

11.8 He/She/It was applauding

11.9 He/She/It was watering the flowers

11.10 He/She/It was spending

11.11 He/She/It was buying

11.12 He/She/It was jumping

11.13 He/She/It was making an announcement

11.14 He/She/It was punching

11.15 He/She/It was pressing

11.16 He/She/It was opening

11.17 He/She/It was smoking

11.18 He/She/It was healing

11.19 He/She/It was preparing

11.20 He/She/It was strengthening

## 12. *Übung*

12.1 Darius was the best!

12.2 Derek cooked the best!

12.3 Babette collected the most!

12.4 The Queen learned a new language the fastest!

12.5 The tomcat ate the most!

## 13. Übung

13.1 Darius hört einem singenden Vogel jetzt schon zwei Stunden zu ...

13.2 Derek träumt schon viele Jahre lang davon, die größte Blume auf Erden zu züchten.

13.3 Babette duscht schon bereits seit drei Uhr und sie hat noch immer nicht das Badezimmer verlassen!

13.4 Drei Kobolde spazieren schon seit zehn Stunden ...

13.5 Die Königin spielt schon viele Jahre lang Flöte.

13.6 Darius und Salyna lachen bereits seit einer halben Stunde ...

## 14. Übung

14.1 Greetings, my friend!

14.2 Please get me the big cauldron from the cellar!

14.3 Leave the town immediately!

14.4 Prepare yourself to fight!

14.5 Don't get upset!

14.6 Good night! I close my eyes, knowing that I'll never be able to enjoy the light of day again.

14.7 The trees here in the forest look very frightening!

14.8 The old woman was a witch then?

14.9 The elders' books are kept in this library.

14.10 I'm so glad that you're coming with me to the orc tribe.

14.11 Your sword is decorated with beautiful precious stones – how much was it?

14.12 This armour offers better resistance against magic because Darius has cast a spell on it!

14.13 I urgently need a new shield made of steel!

14.14 With this crossbow, you cannot fight against the dragon!

14.15 This coat of chainmail is of high quality!

14.16 This is exactly the right thing for me!

14.17 The strange wizard asked Darius if he knew how he was called.

14.18 A beautiful woman who calls herself Julia came to Darius today and asked him for a favour.

14.19 Derek and Babette are celebrating a party.

14.20 The sun is setting!

## 15. Übung

15.1 Schau! So viele Sternschnuppen sind am Himmel!

15.2 Dies ist ein schöner Tag gewesen! Lass uns nächste Woche wieder treffen, ok?

15.3 Ich schwöre, dass ich gerade einen Geist im Keller gesehen habe!

15.4 Bitte glaube mir, ich habe das Buch nicht gestohlen!

15.5 Warum schreist du? Das ist nur eine winzige Spinne!

15.6 Nicht in meinen wildesten Träumen dachte ich, dass dies geschehen könnte!

15.7 Ok, ich werde dich zu meinem Herrn bringen.

15.8 Oh nein! Ein Gewitter! Geht in eure Häuser und bleibt dort, bis das Gewitter fort ist!

15.9 Er soll sie zu mir bringen! Ich möchte selber hören, was sie zu sagen hat.

15.10 Er stand dort, ohne ein Wort zu sagen.

## 16. Übung

16.1 firmly

16.2 excitedly

16.3 weakly

16.4 freshly

16.5 strongly

16.6 carelessly

16.7 offensively

16.8 loudly

16.9 quietly

16.10 high

16.11 cruelly

16.12 happily

16.13 extremely

16.14 warmly

16.15 coldly

16.16 gladly

16.17 carefully

16.18 sadly

16.19 calmly

16.20 brightly

16.21 softly

## 17. Übung

17.1 I will / shall be talking

17.2 I will / shall be playing

17.3 I will / shall be speaking

17.4 I will / shall be working

17.5 I will / shall be writing

17.6 I will / shall be reading

17.7 I will / shall be catching

17.8 I will / shall be barking

17.9 I will / shall be teaching

17.10 I will / shall be traveling

## 18. *Übung*

18.1 He/She/It calls

18.2 He/She/It brings

18.3 He/She/It lies

18.4 He/She/It loves

18.5 He/She/It kisses

18.6 He/She/It dreams

18.7 He/She/It reaches

18.8 He/She/It burns

18.9 He/She/It heats up

18.10 He/She/It smiles

## 19. *Übung*

19.1 Darius fought against a black dragon.

19.2 When did Derek get his first flower?

19.3 Babette has to do a lot of things today.

19.4 How much does this yellow potion cost?

19.5 I'll take the book to the library.

19.6 It is pretty noisy in the marketplace today.

19.7 It's too cold to go swimming in the sea this morning.

19.8 Don't disturb me, please!


## 20. Übung

20.1 Ich weiß wirklich nicht, für was dieser Zauber gut ist.

20.2 Salyna hat soeben eine alte Dame getroffen, die sie schon seit langer Zeit nicht mehr gesehen hatte.

20.3 Tut mir Leid, aber ich weiß nicht, wo sie wohnt.

20.4 Die Orks und zwei Drachen attackieren gerade die Burg!

20.5 Derek schwingt gerade seine Axt.

20.6 Darius ist nicht zu Hause … Das ist seltsam!

20.7 Es ist dir nicht erlaubt, zu passieren!

20.8 Ich hätte nie gedacht, dass ich so eine schöne Robe erstehen könnte.


## 21. Übung

21.1 A stranger entered the town yesterday and hasn't been seen since then.

21.2 I need to buy some magic cloth to make a new robe.

21.3 There's no need for panic!

21.4 It's exactly like that! So, please go to Darius!

21.5 Help us! Our farm is burning!

21.6 If I had taught you the spell, you would have disappeared!

21.7 The Queen was sitting on a bank in the park yesterday while eating chocolate ice cream.

21.8 This potion is most expensive – no, I don't want to buy it!

21.9 Did you even think that you could defeat me?!

21.10 Your grandfather went for a walk in the park and spoke to the birds as if they were men.


## 22. Übung

22.1 Darius liebt es, spät in der Nacht zu baden.

22.2 Babettes allerliebstes Nahrungsmittel ist Schokoladeneis.

22.3 Derek und seine Frau tanzten um Mitternacht in ihrem Garten.

22.4 Derek und Darius sind auf dem Weg zum Haus einer Hexen, welches sich tief im Wald befindet.

22.5 Darius und Babette schwimmen schon seit fünf Uhr morgens im Meer.

22.6 Darius hat noch nie zuvor in einem Drachenhort geschlafen.

22.7 Diese Burg ist sehr alt; einige Leute sagen sogar, dass hier finstere Rituale durchgeführt worden sind.

22.8 Ich erwarte, dass du früh aufstehst, diese Bücher bis fünf Uhr gelesen hast und um acht Uhr ins Bett gehst.

22.9 Bitte verstehe mich nicht falsch … Ich mag dich einfach …

22.10 Versuche nicht einmal, das zu tun! Du wirst es bereuen!

### 23. Übung

23.1 Darius said that he visited the Queen this morning.

23.2 Derek asked Darius to visit him as soon as he had finished his work.

23.3 Derek and Babette asked Darius if he knew where one could find rare flowers.

23.4 Darius and Derek asked the stranger where he wanted to go.

23.5 Darius suggested not starting a war with the orcs.

23.6 The Queen suggested sending nine knights to the abandoned estate.

23.7 Darius thought that he would not survive that night.

23.8 Darius and Derek thought that the Queen would not meet with the leader of the orcs.

23.9 Derek asked his wife if she could bring a mug with cool water to him.

23.10 Darius said that he wouldn't have gone into the lake at such a late hour.


## 24. Übung

24.1 weaker

24.2 stronger

24.3 healthier

24.4 bigger

24.5 shorter

24.6 older

24.7 younger

24.8 deeper

24.9 higher

24.10 clearer

## 25. Übung

25.1 stiffest

25.2 most tired

25.3 easiest

25.4 hardest

25.5 sunniest

25.6 darkest

25.7 brightest

25.8 loudest

25.9 most elastic

25.10 cleanest

## 26. Übung

26.1 Darius is the best wizard I know.

26.2 Babette seems to be pretty satisfied with her newly bought shoes.

26.3 Darius has never seen a black dragon again.

26.4 A necromancer was seen in the abandoned castle just a few minutes ago.

26.5 Derek had been watering the beautiful flowers since that morning.

26.6 Darius can't stand Mister Gnom's behaviour today.

26.7 Dear Ms Babette, have you received my letter?

26.8 Go deeper into the cave, and you'll find the treasure for sure!

26.9 Don't you dare touch my butt!

26.10 This skeleton is pretty creepy!


### 27. Übung

27.1 helped

27.2 made, potion

27.3 control

27.4 fertilizer

27.5 ghost

27.6 mind

27.7 find

27.8 talked

27.9 naked

27.10 keep


## 28. *Übung*

28.1 when

28.2 where

28.3 how

28.4 what

28.5 why

28.6 what

28.7 how

28.8 why

28.9 where

28.10 when

## 29. Übung

29.1 Darius war der Erste, der diese Art von Trank erfunden hat.

29.2 Es ist erstaunlich, wie schnell diese Kreaturen herumfliegen können!

29.3 Entschuldigung, könnten Sie mir bitte den Weg zu Sir Almonds Herrenhaus zeigen?

29.4 Sir Excellus las gewöhnlich ein Buch über Geschichte, wenn ich ihn in der Bibliothek sah.

29.5 Nein, Magie ist nicht das Richtige – weder für ein kleines Mädchen noch für einen Jungen – es ist zu gefährlich.

29.6 Alchemie ist schwer zu erlernen.

29.7 Mit diesem Zauber ist es mir möglich, Schneeflocken größer zu machen!

29.8 Möchtest du ein kühles Getränk, Darius?

29.9 Angenommen, es gäbe keine Sterne – wie würdest du dich fühlen?

29.10 Ich wünschte, ich wüsste ihren Namen ...

## 30. Übung

30.1 Look at this mess! A stupid imp has devastated my whole laboratory!

30.2 I don't believe you! It was you who reanimated the dead and destroyed the village!

30.3 May you find a way to drive the evil out of this hall.

30.4 The dream was so real … I'm wondering if it really was just a dream ...

30.5 Would you like to go with me to the fortress of the magic knights?

30.6 Imps may not be very clever, but they are very amusing.

30.7 I'll have taught you the art of alchemy before I die.

30.8 Believe in your heart!

30.9 I'm so happy because I've learned my first spell today!

30.10 You are very brave! I think that I couldn't have put the troll to flight.